Christine Merrill lives on a farm in Wisconsin, USA, with her husband, two sons and too many pets—all of whom would like her to get off the computer so they can check their e-mail. She has worked by turns in theatre costuming and as a librarian. Writing historical romance combines her love of good stories and fancy dress with her ability to stare out of the window and make stuff up.

VOWS TO SAVE HER REPUTATION

Christine Merrill

MILLS & BOON

First published in Great Britain 2020
by Mills & Boon, an imprint of HarperCollins*Publishers*
1 London Bridge Street, London, SE1 9GF

Large Print edition 2020

© 2020 Christine Merrill

ISBN: 978-0-263-08660-7

MIX
Paper from
responsible sources
FSC™ C007454

This book is produced from independently certified FSC™ paper to ensure responsible forest management. For more information visit www.harpercollins.co.uk/green.

Printed and bound in Great Britain
by CPI Group (UK) Ltd, Croydon, CR0 4YY

To Jim, a very patient man.

Chapter One

Emma Harris looked longingly out the morning room window at the sun shining on the park of her father's country estate. It was a perfect day for a stroll. It would be nice just to sit beneath a tree and finish her book. Or she could take her sketchbook instead and draw mediocre charcoals of the little animals scurrying across the lawn. There were many ways she might occupy the space between now and luncheon that were either pleasurable or edifying.

But she would have happily stood in a downpour and done nothing at all rather than to be trapped here with her mother, undergoing the same quizzing that she got each day, as Mrs Harris tried unsuccessfully to turn her into the daughter the family wanted her to be.

'Lord Weatherly,' her mother intoned, staring at the piece of paper in her hand.

'Baron,' Emma replied, automatically.

'Marital status?'

'Never wed at forty-five,' Emma replied. There were probably reasons that he had escaped women thus far. It was unlikely that the cause was homeliness, for she doubted that anyone who had risen to the rank of baron would be deemed too ugly to marry. It was probably temperament. She had met several of the men on her mother's precious list and found some of them to be bordering on misogynistic.

'Hobbies?' her mother prompted.

She could not, for the life of her, remember. In such cases, it was safe to guess, 'Horses.'

'Horticulture,' her mother said with a frown of disapproval.

'I always mix those two up,' she said with a sigh.

'They have nothing in common other than the first letter,' her mother said. 'It is not confusion. It is evidence that you have not been studying the information I have gathered for you. Honestly, my dear, we shall never get you a husband if you are not willing to put in the effort necessary to catch one.

Though it was possible she was wrong, Emma doubted that other young ladies who sought husbands were forced to memorise the names and descriptions of eligible men. 'Can I not just meet them naturally, as strangers, and find out the details later in an organic development of our acquaintance?'

'You could if your father had a title to match theirs,' her mother replied. 'Of course, then you would already know them. You would have vouchers for Almack's and arranged introductions. But your father has a stocking factory. Since you have money rather than breeding, we expect you to work harder to overcome the artificial distance that society has placed between you and the husband you deserve.' Mother always spoke as if being rich somehow entitled the family to the privileges normally afforded to people of rank.

'I could always marry a man in trade,' Emma said, trying not to sound too hopeful. In truth, she did not particularly want to marry at all. The last thing she needed was some strange man correcting her many flaws in a way that might be even more critical than her mother's. But her mother seemed dead set on a match this year and on yoking her to a man with a pedigree.

'We did not raise you to marry a cit,' her mother said, as if it had been possible to breed her for matrimonial success. 'If we had, we would not have wasted money on educating you. We wish for you to better yourself.'

That made no sense. If she married, she would not be better. She could be the same, overly tall, clumsy, daughter of a stocking maker that she had always been. But if the right husband could be caught, she would be Lady something instead of plain Emma. And according to her father, when one wished to sell a product, having the right label mattered even more than the contents of the box.

At least, that was all that mattered to her mother, who was referring to her list again, then looking back to Emma with a raised eyebrow. 'You will have no husband at all if you do not do the work necessary to know who is available and who is not, so that you might cultivate the right people when you meet them. Now, tell me about Lord Braxton.'

This one was easy. 'Engaged,' she said with triumph. 'The announcement was in *The Times* this week.'

Her mother said an unladylike word under her breath and reached for a pen to cross the name from her list. 'I had such hopes for him.'

Emma had felt nothing but dread at the idea. The man was over sixty and had buried three wives already. 'It is unfortunate,' she said, hoping to mollify her mother.

'Worse than that,' she countered. 'That is the third loss this month.' She spoke as if the men belonged to her, like a flock of unruly chickens that kept escaping before they could be butchered and brought to table.

'There will be other years,' Emma said, crossing her fingers.

'For you?' Her mother gave her a dubious look that was most disheartening. 'Your major advantage is that you are young. You are also…robust.' It was a most unfeminine word to describe her, but her mother probably thought she had found a charitable term to describe a girl who was nearly six foot tall. 'Not every man is willing to have a wife taller than himself.' Then, she spoiled what little compliment she had offered. 'You are young, but youth is a fleeting thing, my dear.'

'Mama, I am only one and twenty.'

'And next year, you shall be twenty-two.' She said it in a dire tone that implied her death was imminent. 'There are still a few names left. Tell me about Sir Robert Gascoyne.'

'Thirty-two and widowed. A baronet. Brother of Jack Gascoyne, the war hero. Possessor of an estate not two miles from here.'

'And…' her mother said significantly.

'There is little more to tell. The man is practically a hermit.'

'He has the nicest house in the county,' her mother prompted. 'Twenty acres and nearly as many rooms in the manor. Just think of the parties you will have there, should you marry him.'

'Should he offer for me,' Emma corrected. 'Which I doubt he shall, since we have yet to meet him in person at any of the gatherings in the public assembly halls we have been to. He does not go to the balls in London, nor does he entertain in his own home.

And I have yet to meet a single person who can claim his acquaintance.'

'That will change, once he is married,' her mother insisted. 'You will have a ball and invite titled ladies and gentlemen. In return, they shall invite you to their homes. He might stay at home as much as he wishes, but you, my dear, will be a success. And when you are, I hope that you will remember your poor mother and make introductions.'

'Of course,' Emma said weakly. As the months of the season had passed, her mother had grown more and more obsessed with the idea of finding a way into the aristocracy for their family. Her current strategy involved Emma's successful marriage. Perhaps it was lack of effort on her part, as her mother claimed. Or perhaps she was simply not wanted. Thus far, all those careful plans had been unsuccessful.

'Study the list.' Her mother pressed the paper into her hands with a sense of urgency. 'Knowledge is the key to everything.'

'I will, Mama,' she said, tucking it into the back of the novel she had been reading. 'But for now, I think a walk is in order, if I wish to continue in robust good health.'

'Then walk in the direction of the Gascoyne house and see if you can find a way to meet our neighbour Sir Robert,' she said with a firm nod. 'All you need is one happy accident with the right gentleman and you shall have maids calling you My Ladyship by Christmas.'

Sir Robert Gascoyne liked his solitude.

Rather, he tolerated it, as one would an old and somewhat tiresome friend. He had been alone for so long that he could not think of any other way to be.

Since it did not make him actively unhappy, he told himself that it was for the best that he remained secluded. When one had the luck of the Gascoyne family, it was better to live in isolation as one would when suffering from a disease. Self-quarantine spared the people around him from contagious misfortune.

Though that plan spared others, for Robert there was no escaping the family curse. According to his man of business in London, though every other mine in Cornwall flourished, the tin mine he had invested in had run out of ore. While he had been to visit it, his coachman had been kicked by a horse and broken a leg.

And yet, it could have been worse.

He must be thankful that he was still healthy enough to drive himself home, rather than leaving his best carriage in the hands of inexperienced grooms. With his finances in ruins and his strategies in chaos, it felt good to be in the driver's seat and not dependent on the actions of another. He needed something he could successfully command to steady his nerves and to allow him to believe, for a few hours at least, that his life and destiny were something he could control, as easily as he could command a team and carriage.

The trip thus far had been uneventful. He was an excellent driver more than capable of handling any equipage. The horses were receptive to every flick of the reins. If the wheels stayed on the brougham, he would be home in less than an hour.

That was why he looked at the woman on the road ahead with trepidation. The way was wide enough for a pedestrian and she was well over to the side. There was no reason to believe that she was at risk from him. But there had been no reason to believe that a productive mine could lose the vein right after he had put money down on it. When Robert Gascoyne was involved, bad things happened.

As he approached her, he pulled as far to the opposite side of the road as he thought safe and slowed to a trot. Since she appeared to be absorbed in the book she was reading, he called to the groom to blow a warning on the carriage horn.

Perhaps he had waited too long to make his presence known. At the sound, she gave a start of alarm and so did the horses. The team shied and, as he struggled to control them, he lost sight of her. One minute she was there, the next she had disappeared from sight.

Robert felt a moment of blind panic as he tugged hard on the reins, cursing his carelessness and infernal bad luck, and hating each movement of hooves that might be further trampling the poor girl. The lack of cries was an ominous silence which made him wonder if she'd been killed outright by the first blow.

But, no. When he was able to hop down, she was not under the horses, but laying in a heap at the bottom of the ditch beside the road, face down and dangerously close to a puddle.

He stumbled down the hill after her, praying that he was not already too late as he rolled her face towards the sky. God bless her, though unconscious, she was still breathing. Her fair looks had survived quite well under a coating of muck and despite the cut on her forehead that was releasing a steady trickle of blood, vibrant red against her coppery hair.

'Miss?' he said gently, not wanting to startle her again. But the word did not earn even a moan of response. The pulse where he touched her hand was weak and her gown was torn in several places, a sign of the battering she had taken on the tumble downhill. She needed cold compresses for the bruises and someone more skilled than he to identify further injuries.

He dropped her fallen book into his pocket and scooped her into his arms, then laboured up the hill, surprised at her height which must be near to his own when she was capable of standing. Hopefully, this giantess would have stamina worthy of her size and shake off her injuries as quickly as she'd encountered them.

But for now, what was he to do with her? The village would be the more proper destination. But if there was something seriously wrong with her, his home was several miles closer and nearer to the surgeon's home as well. He would see to her welfare first. Then, with luck she would come round enough so that he could establish her identity and send someone for her people.

With a sigh of frustration, he carried her to the carriage and laid her down on one of the seats, signalling to a groom to take the reins for the last few miles to the house, before climbing in beside her and resting her head on his lap.

As they travelled, he fixed his eyes on the opposite wall, trying to ignore the strange, unsettled feeling of having a woman so close in the privacy of the carriage. It had been a long time since he'd been alone with any sort of female and even longer since his needs had been met by one. It was wrong to even think about such things in the presence of a well-born young lady, but he could not seem to turn his mind away from them.

He glanced down at her, then quickly away again. She was not the prettiest girl in England, but she was certainly one of the most striking he had seen. Would her eyes be blue or green when she opened them? Either would be an appealing match to her hair.

If she opened them, he reminded himself, reaching into his pocket and finding a handkerchief, then splashing some brandy from his flask on to it so he could clean the wound on her head. Her skin was pale, but he suspected it was naturally so. Redheads often had the sort of luminous complexion that this woman did. Even smudged with dirt, there was an almost regal dignity about her that was clearly a sign of excellent breeding. She put him in mind of a sleeping princess, albeit a very tall one.

He could not help casting a glance at her left hand and its empty ring finger. He was not in the market for a wife, now or ever. Nor was he the prince that this girl deserved.

After seeing what damage he could do in a wordless meeting, she would be wise to run from him before they had spoken. Since she was unable to escape, it would be his responsibility to keep her safe and free of his company.

But a part of him did not want to. He liked the feeling of her resting against him. It also helped to know that, although he had been responsible for her accident, he was doing his best to make things right again. It went against his nature to leave the work to others, if there was something he could do to help.

Perhaps it was simply because she was young and pretty, but he wanted to be the one who could help this girl. He could imagine her waking, her golden lashes fluttering and the puzzled look on her face turning to relief as he explained that he had rescued her. Then, he would assure her that everything would be right from this point on, for both of them.

He shook his head, rejecting the misguided idea that a happy future would come, just because he wished for it. Then, he reached behind him and opened the window that communicated with the driver and urged the groom on the seat to go faster, so they might arrive home before he had any more foolish ideas.

Chapter Two

Emma awoke with an ache in her head and a sense of dread that began before she had even opened her eyes. Something was very wrong. The smells, the feel, the sounds and everything else about where she was lying were unfamiliar. Try as she might to uncover it, she had no recollection of how she had come to be wherever it was she had ended up.

She struggled to think. She had been reading a most enjoyable novel by Ann of Swansea. It had engrossed her to such a degree that she'd been unable to put it down, even as she went out for the walk to escape from her mother's hectoring. It was why she had not been paying attention when she had moved to the side of the road to let a carriage pass. She would have been better served to have watched the ground, which had seemed to give way beneath one foot, leaving the other on solid purchase.

She rolled her left ankle experimentally and winced. She doubted it was broken. But the rabbit hole, or whatever it was she had stepped in, had given it a good wrenching that would make it impossible to walk without help for several days.

She opened her eyes and raised her head as best as she was able to see the offending extremity propped on a pillow and efficiently bandaged to reduce the swelling. Then she felt up and down her body and found an assortment of fresh bruises, and the surprising and somewhat worrisome knowledge that she was attired in nothing but a shift, in the bed of a stranger.

She raised herself up on her elbows, then dropped back into the pillows again, waiting for the pain in her skull to subside. It was clear that the fall that had caused the sprain had ended with her head against a rock. She could feel a knot on her forehead that was tender to the touch.

It was just as well she could not see it. It was probably ugly. When she got home, she

would get a strong scolding for ending her
chances this season by rendering herself too
hideous for men to consider and unable to
dance due to her own clumsiness. It was just
as well she was not there yet, for it meant her
mother could not see her smiling over what
should have been heartbreaking misfortune.
With luck, she would be able to convince her
father that she needed several weeks of recu-
peration in the country, alone with a stack of
Minerva novels.

'Are you awake, miss?' A maid popped her
head in the doorway. 'The doctor will be so
relieved.'

'A doctor was called?' Now she sat up, despite the pain. 'That was hardly necessary
over a few bruises.'

'Sir Robert insisted,' the maid said.

'Sir Robert Gascoyne?' she said, slinking
back into the pile of pillows, her good mood
forgotten. Mother would be overjoyed that
she had found a way to force herself into the
house of the recluse. But for herself, she was
mortified.

'He has been worried as well,' the maid assured her.

'And I suppose my parents have been summoned,' she said, trying not to sigh.

'We did not know who they were for the longest time,' the maid said.

'Longest time? How long have I been here?' she said, confused.

'For two days.' This was said in a hushed tone that implied it was the most exciting thing to happen in ages. 'The doctor said it was best not to try to wake you to ask, but we could find nothing to tell us who you were. Sir Robert sent men to the village to discover whether any ladies were missing. But it was not until this morning…'

'My parents did not miss me?' she said, surprised.

'They have just arrived and are speaking with the master,' the maid assured her.

That did not explain why they had not been looking for her yesterday. But Emma had a horrible feeling that she knew. 'I certainly hope they are bringing me a clean gown,' she said, looking down at her shift. 'This is rather improper.'

'We tried, but there was nothing to be done for the one you were wearing,' the maid replied with a sad shake of her head. 'And there was nothing in this house that would fit you.'

'Of course not,' she said, used to the inconvenience her height inflicted.

'When Sir Robert carried you into the house, your gown was hanging off you in tatters,' the maid said, fluffing the pillow behind her head. 'And he swept up the stairs with you and set you down on the bed as if you weighed no more than a feather.'

It was a romantic exaggeration. It had to be. 'Has Sir Robert been to see me since?' she said hesitantly, trying not to imagine the poor man struggling under her weight. 'Perhaps you could summon him. I would like to apologise for imposing on him in this way.'

At this, the maid giggled. 'It was him what imposed on you, miss, running you off the road as he did.'

'He was driving the carriage?' she questioned.

'There had been an earlier accident,' the maid replied, as if that made any sense at all. 'But he was most worried about you.'

'That is very kind of him,' she replied, wondering if the gentleman himself might be able to shed any light on what had happened. 'Will I be allowed to meet my rescuer?' she repeated. 'I wish to thank him.'

'He says it would not be proper, what with you being in a bedchamber and all,' the maid said. 'But I am sure you can write him, after you have gone home.'

'Of course,' Emma answered weakly, wondering how big a failure she was at husband hunting that she could not manage to meet a man even while staying in his house.

'Or you can meet him in a few minutes, after you are properly dressed,' her mother said from the doorway. Then she pushed past the maid and into the room, coming to the bed to take Emma's hands and inspect her critically. 'I have a fresh gown for you and some hair ribbons. But I suppose there is nothing to be done about the bruises.'

As expected, she had disappointed, yet again. 'My ankle is twisted, as well. But the rest of me does not feel so very bad, from the inside.' That was a lie. The pounding from the bump on her head made her want to crawl back under the covers and hide. Or was it just the presence of her mother? Surely Emma's stomach had not been in knots a few moments ago. Nor had her hands felt like trembling.

'You fall down often enough to know your own mind on the subject of personal injury,' her mother said with a resigned sigh. 'But this time we need you to rise up quickly and make a proper impression on the man who saved your life.'

'It is good that he was there to notice me stumble,' Emma replied, marshalling her courage. 'From what I understand, you and father misplaced me.'

'Do not be ridiculous. One of our footmen was a mile down the road and saw you being taken into Sir Robert's carriage. He was too far away to help, but he informed us of what had happened, immediately. We knew you were safe all along,' her mother admitted, showing no sign of real guilt that she had done nothing with the knowledge.

'Then why did you leave me here?'

'Once we understood where he had taken you, we decided it would be better to wait until morning to see about claiming you.' Then, her mother gave a sly smile. 'Because of the unfortunate delay, your father is speaking with Sir Robert, even as I am speaking to you.'

There was a confusing significance to her tone, and Emma wondered what it was that she was missing about the exchange. It seemed there was a new plan in place and once again she was at the centre of it. But for the life of her, she could not guess what it might be. 'Why don't we all speak to Sir Robert?' she suggested in a warning tone. 'I should like to thank him for the care he has given to me. It was most kind of him to extend compassion to a stranger. But I would not want him to get the impression that we are seeking an advantage over him.' She needed to show him the respect that he deserved so that he did not regret that he had helped her at all. Her father, with his exceptionally blunt nature, was likely to leave him thinking that the neighbours were both nosy and rude.

'He was very kind to take care of you. Yet, unwise,' her mother said with a sad nod that had not a hint of sincerity in it. 'You resided here for two days with no chaperon.'

'I have not needed one,' she insisted. 'I was

unconscious the whole time and have not got into any trouble at all.'

'The bruises will heal, but your reputation never shall,' her mother reminded her, with a heavy sigh but a twinkle in her eye. 'And, as your father is conveying to Sir Robert, there is only one way to make things right.'

Emma tried and failed to think what it might be. One hardly expected the fellow to apologise for not leaving an injured woman in a ditch. Then the fog in her head cleared for a moment and she remembered she was speaking to the woman who had written that infernal list. 'You are not speaking of marriage, are you?' She forced a laugh and prayed that her mother would join her in it.

Instead, her statement was greeted with an enthusiastic nod.

'Is that why father is speaking to Sir Robert?' she said, alarmed.

'He would not accept any of our other invitations,' her mother reminded her. 'Nor would he come out of his house to be met in a normal way.'

But that did not mean he deserved to be forced into marriage with the first stranger who fell at his feet. 'You and Father must stop this nonsense this instant.' Emma did her best to bolt out of bed, only to have the pain in her ankle remind her that it was impossible. It was only with a show of fortitude on her part that the endeavour ended in her flopping back on the bed and not landing in a heap on the floor.

'Do not be silly, darling,' her mother soothed, helping her to sit up. 'Leave the men to settle things between them and you will be married before you know it.'

'That is the last thing I was hoping,' she said, struggling upright with the support of a bedpost. She held out a hand. 'Give me my gown and a hairbrush. Once I am dressed, we will go downstairs and apologise for the imposition. Then we shall go home and never speak of this again.'

In the study below, Robert was beginning to wonder if he was the one who had received a head wound and not the unfortunate girl in the bed above stairs. It appeared his poor luck was holding true as ever. What had started as a simple act of charity had resulted in more trouble than he could ever have imagined.

Of course, that charity would not have been necessary if he hadn't run the girl down. If they'd never met, she'd have avoided injury altogether. Perhaps he did owe her something. But surely not the marriage her father seemed to be hinting at.

'You must admit that there is no other way,' the man said in an annoyingly reasonable voice.

'I damn well won't,' Robert snapped. 'She has been in the house but two days.'

'Two days,' the other intoned, as if it were six months in a hareem. 'Would it not have made more sense to take her to the inn to lessen the risk to her honour?'

'I would have risked her health instead,' Robert said, cursing the nonsensical rules placed on the young ladies of the country and his own faulty logic in choosing home over a more public place to house her.

'Her health will heal. But a good reputation, once lost, cannot be regained,' her father bemoaned.

'She was perfectly safe here,' Robert countered. 'I have not so much as crossed the threshold to her room.'

'But who would know that?' Mr Harris said patiently.

'My servants,' he insisted.

'Who would lie for their master, if you asked them to,' Harris said.

'The doctor.'

'Also in your employ,' Harris answered. 'And he is widely known as a drinker.'

'He is?' Robert said, surprised. The man had been in attendance at his late wife's childbed, though he did not think he could blame the physician for what had resulted then.

'But you, Sir Robert?' the stranger continued. 'The people of the town do not know enough to vouch for your character, since they never see you outside of this house, nor are any allowed inside.'

'Because I am not running a roadside inn. I prefer solitude to company,' he replied. It sounded petulant, but his real reasons sounded even worse.

'But such behaviour has done nothing to scotch the rumours that have spread over the area about the things that must occur in this house if you are so eager to hide from them.' Harris added a tsk and a regretful shake of the head.

'Nothing goes on here,' he snapped again. He could hardly afford the sort of debauchery that idle minds could imagine, but it was also true that he had done nothing to replace those wild rumours with truth.

'And it is not as if there will not be a substantial settlement made upon you, after the wedding,' the father of this complete stranger replied to him.

Against all that he wished to feel, Robert's spirit lifted in hope. He had known that marrying well was a possible solution to his financial problems. He had always rejected it because he could not imagine himself married again. Nor did he want to risk the life of an innocent woman by subjecting her to the sort of ill fortune that would invariably fall upon her, should she become his wife.

But that care had been for women not already trapped by fate and all but thrown into his path. It was beginning to appear that it was already too late for Emma Harris to escape a permanent association with him.

The least he could do was minimise the immediate damage he had done. That it would benefit him as well might be the first fortunate coincidence of his life.

'How big a settlement, precisely?' he said, feeling his gut churn at the commonness of such a question.

'I run a successful group of stocking factories in the north,' the fellow said. 'The young lady upstairs is worth easily twenty thousand a year to the man who marries her. Since she has no brother, she will be worth considerably more than that on my death.'

For a moment, distaste was replaced with a flash of avarice. Then, common sense returned to remind him that it might as well have been a sentence of murder to wed the girl, so likely was she to die in childbed, just as his last wife had and generations of Gascoyne women before her.

There is an easy enough way to avoid children, said an equally sensible voice. *You have but to avoid her bed.*

Since they had never spoken, he doubted that she was pining to lie with him and he certainly held no carnal feelings when he thought of her.

Not many, at least. She was pretty, of course. But he was a man of reason, capable of resisting the temptations of the flesh, if he put his mind to it. And what her father was suggesting was more of a business transaction than a marriage.

'Will your daughter agree with this?' he said, still surprised by the suddenness of this offer. 'She has not yet seen me, much less talked to me.'

'Her mother is speaking with her now,' her father said with a nod. 'By the time you go to her with your offer, it will already be arranged.'

Arranged. He liked the word for it was a good way to describe the sort of marriage they would have. It would be an arrangement. He would be a respectful, if unaffectionate, husband and his title would open doors to her that she could never have breached on her own. His offer, if he made it, would be generosity itself and would give her a future far nicer than she might have as the wife of a cit.

'Let me call for brandy and you can tell me

more,' Robert said, hoping the drink would wash away the feeling that he was trading himself, body, soul and title, to a stranger.

Chapter Three

A short while later, Emma Harris was still bruised and broken. But she was also combed and primped and, according to her mother, ready to meet the man she was to marry.

She felt rather like the sleeping princess in the fairy tale who had woken not just to a handsome prince but a readymade family, complete with twins and no say in the matter at all.

She'd never seen anything particularly romantic about that story, since it was clear that the prince in it had taken advantage of a helpless woman. If that was the best that romance had to offer, Emma would have just as soon stayed asleep.

To the best of her knowledge, Sir Robert Gascoyne had been a perfect gentleman to her in the time she'd spent in his house. But the man must be a halfwit if he was willing to be talked into an offer without talking to her first.

Or perhaps he was only a fortune hunter. Despite her reluctance to marry, the prospect of meeting one of those was rather exciting. Though the family money was prodigious, thus far it had not been enough to persuade the gentleman she'd met to overlook her gracelessness and come up to scratch.

But none of that mattered now. If Sir Robert was unwilling to put a stop to the nonsense that her parents had arranged, then she would have to do it for him. If and when an offer came, she had but to give him a polite no and thank him for his care of her. It was the sensible thing to do.

Then the bedroom door opened and her father and her host entered. And she decided that good sense did not matter so very much, when one was presented with a man who looked like Sir Robert Gascoyne.

Dear God, but he was beautiful, miles above the horrid choices that her family had suggested thus far. They had proven to care more about the titles of the gentlemen they chose for her than whether there was any suitability between the parties involved. It meant that she had been picking through the castoffs of the social season: men who were old, ugly and poor, and no more interested in her than she was in them.

But Sir Robert was none of those things. If he had such a beautiful home, he could not be too very poor. He was also young and strapping. If he had attempted to take advantage of her at any time during the last two days, her only regret was that she had not been awake to enjoy it. The thought made her wish she was holding a fan and could flutter it as a diversion while she catalogued his virtues. Instead, all she could do was stare.

His hair was an unruly chestnut and looked as if it wanted trimming. There was a matching stubble forming on the hollows of his perfect cheekbones that hinted he did not bother with a razor when guests were not expected.

His dress confirmed her suspicion of carelessness, for though his clothes were immaculate with a well-tailored coat and crisp white linen, one of the shiny buttons on his sleeve was loose, falling noticeably out of line with its fellows. It seemed that his valet had gone through the motions of brushing and pressing and lost interest before he'd finished the job.

It made Emma wonder what other corners she might find that had been cut, should she take a proper inventory of the staff and their work. Clearly, the man was in need of a wife, if only to civilise his habits and organise his household.

But the problems with his grooming were almost a relief, since they were the only things keeping him from an unattainable perfection. His eyes were the green of China jade, clear and alert. His brow was furrowed, but wide and intelligent. His shadowed cheekbones were high and his nose straight and aristocratic.

But most exciting of all, he was tall. He stood at least a head above her last suitor and, even if she were standing, to look him in the eye she would have to raise her chin. Not much, of course, but it had been so long since she'd done it for anyone that her neck cracked with the effort. It did not exactly make her feel small, but looking up at this man was a delicious taste of how other girls must feel all the time.

This interview would be easier if he was not so very pretty. Then, perhaps, she could remind herself how ludicrous the situation was. They could both laugh at the idea of marriage, just as she had planned to in the first place. He could go back to his study and she could go home and this meeting would be nothing more than an unpleasant memory.

But now that she had seen him, she wanted to sit here, staring at him, listening to the sound of his voice, which was deep and soothing, like the booming of a distant storm just as one was drifting off. If she could hear him speak a few hours before bed each night, she was sure that she would sleep better for it.

Perhaps he could recite verse. There was something about the louche knot in his cravat that made her think of a dissolute poet. But she doubted that he was truly dissipated. There was no sign of excess in his face or frame.

He looked sad, rather than unhealthy. He just needed someone to cheer him up. He was too sombre. And she was known in her very small circle of friends as having an excellent sense of humour.

Then she realised that she was sitting on the edge of the bed, staring at him as he talked, but not hearing a word of what he was saying. She had missed the introductions entirely. And if the proposal had been wonderful, terrible or non-existent, she had not heard a word of it.

She doubted that it was the stuff of dreams, for she did not think that a man who had been forced into offering would be up to climbing the stairs and wooing her as if there were anything normal about this situation.

He had stopped talking and she had not even noticed. Now, his expression was one of barely contained annoyance, as he waited for her answer.

'Yes?' she said, unable to keep the question from her voice. Then, she remembered that she had meant to say no. She was not as foolish as to believe in love at first sight. But neither could she deny that it had taken one look at him for her good judgement to fly out the window.

Perhaps it was good that she had a bump

on her head. She would rather he think that the way she was behaving might have something to do with damage to the brain than normal stupidity. It might not be too late to retract her acceptance, claiming headache and confusion. But she could not seem to get her mouth to form any words at all.

'Very well then,' he said, when it was apparent to everyone in the room that she was not going to say anything more. 'I will arrange for the special licence and call for you at your parents' home in one week's time. I trust you will be sufficiently healed by then to visit the vicar.'

'Of course,' she said, wishing that she could flip back through the conversation, like the pages in a book, and start it again. Then she might at least manage to be clever and to leave him with a better impression of herself.

Instead, she was passive and silent as she was helped into a chair that the servants carried down the stairs and out of the door to her parents' waiting carriage.

Conscience was a malleable thing, but it had an annoying habit of springing back to its original position without warning. Robert almost succeeded in remaining silent for the entire week. But at six days—one before his impromptu wedding—he surrendered to the nagging voice in his head that insisted it was unfair to marry any woman without giving her some idea of what her future with him might be.

She had said yes, another voice argued. That one word was all that was required. Any further negotiation was done with parents, not the young women.

But then he remembered that she had given that consent with a tone of surprise that hinted at the same confusion he had felt when considering the prospect of marriage. Her father had promised him that she understood and agreed with the plan. But the poor thing had still been dazed by her injury when he'd made his proposal, barely in her right mind enough to make an answer.

He had taken advantage of the fact and withheld information. The knowledge raised an unease that grew with each passing minute, plaguing him to tell her, lest the secret drive him mad. There was no way that he could go through a ceremony without setting things straight between them.

If she was decided, there should be no harm to the contract in speaking to her before it was carried out. But if she was having doubts, she deserved the right to be well informed on her future and set free, should she wish. So, he saddled a horse and rode out to unburden his soul.

The home that Harris had rented was a new-ish manor house, probably well designed and full of the sorts of modern improvements that his own servants would have appreciated, had he been able to afford renovations. Wanting after such things was what had driven him to agree to Harris's offer of a dowried daughter. He did not precisely regret it, now. He simply wished that finances had not been such a big part of his motive for choosing a wife.

His future father-in-law had come by his money from honest labour. That was a path denied a gentleman, who was expected to keep his hands unsullied by work even if it meant empty pockets. But pushing a girl to marry him and solve his problems seemed less honourable rather than more so.

When he presented himself at the front door and announced his desire to speak to his fiancée in private, Mrs Harris declared it improper. Her husband simply found it odd. The deal was done. What was the point of discussing it afterwards?

'If we are going to be husband and wife in less than a day, what harm can it do to an honour you claim I have already besmirched?' Robert said with some impatience.

At this, they relented and he was shown to a receiving room, where, a short time later, Miss Harris appeared. He could still see the shadow of a bruise on her temple from where she had fallen and there was a cautiousness to her step as if her ankle was still feeling weak. Other than that, she seemed a quite ordinary young lady, much like others he had admired before choosing his last wife. Her height was impressive, of course. But it made him think of saplings and their ability to weather storms that might snap reeds.

Still, it was unfair to plant this particular tree in a place of danger without a word of warning to her.

'Sir Robert,' she said softly. 'You wished

to speak with me?' She dropped an unsteady curtsy, then rose again, as quickly as she was able, clasping her hands together as if she was not quite sure what to do with them.

'Miss Harris,' he replied, bowing. 'I felt that it was important that we talked, before the ceremony, so that you might be aware of certain things that we did not have the opportunity to discuss, before the proposal.'

'The circumstances were abrupt,' she agreed. The words held a note of censure, but her nervous smile did not falter and the tone did not vary from the same polite alto she had used with him before.

'Your father made it clear to me that honour required a quick decision,' he reminded her.

'I suspect mine would have survived,' she said in an offhand manner. 'When a large settlement is involved, virtue can be strained to cover infractions far greater than a fall in a neighbour's ditch.'

So, she was aware of the power of money. How could she not be? And that meant she must know why he was marrying her. He felt another wave of shame at what he was going to tell her next.

'Despite what you and your family believe, there are limits to what can be bought,' he said, not bothering to be gentle.

'And you are about to tell me what they are,' she said. It was good to know that, should she choose to accept him, his new wife was no fool.

'First, there are things you must know about me and my family, things that I did not tell you when I proposed,' he said. 'You could not possibly make an informed decision tomorrow, if I did not tell you of the truth today.'

'An informed decision,' she repeated with a smile. 'Marriage is quite different for men than it is for women, and there is the proof. Ladies are told to leave the thinking to their parents, Sir Robert, and to never trust their own minds in a matter as important as who they should wed. But if you have things you must tell me, then go to it.'

'The family you are about to join has been cursed with generations of bad luck. Once we are married, you will no doubt receive your share of it.'

To this, she said nothing, simply raising a doubtful eyebrow. She did not believe him.

He hoped she would not learn the truth by bitter experience, as he had.

'When the Gascoynes are involved, crops fail, cattle take sick and businesses founder. The women die in childbed and the men die young for a host of reasons. My grandfather was killed in a carriage accident and my father by suicide after losing most of the family fortune at the gaming tables.'

'Many families have such stories,' she said, unimpressed.

'I have just lost the rest of my money in a sound investment that would have profited greatly had any other man made it,' he said.

'It was why you needed the settlement,' she said.

'When your father suggested marriage, it seemed like a reasonable way forward.'

She nodded in agreement. 'I was not expecting a love match, if that was what you were thinking.'

'Of course not,' he agreed, hurriedly, then continued. 'But as I mentioned before, there is one way that the curse falls more heavily on the women of the family than the men. A Gascoyne bride has not survived childbirth in five generations. I can show you the records in my family bible. It has been one hundred and fifty years, at least, since the wife of a Gascoyne has lived to raise her child.'

'And yet, you have a brother,' she said.

'A half-brother,' he replied. 'My mother died, as did his. The only mothering we received was from our father's third wife, who had no children of her own and no real interest in the pair of us.'

'An unfortunate coincidence,' she replied. Apparently, she was a rationalist.

'Yet I do not want to see a similar *coincidence* carried out again, in my lifetime,' he said. 'I have lost one wife already, and a child as well. I have no desire to risk such a loss again.'

'You do not want children,' she said, clearly shocked at the idea.

'Not if I am destined to lose them or you in trying for them,' he said.

'And you are here to give me the chance to refuse the marriage, based on a decision that could change, later.'

'It will not,' he insisted. 'I am adamant. Just as I planned, before I met you, I will not father a child on you or any other woman. My estate will go to my brother, should he survive me, which he likely will.'

'Because of your luck,' she said.

'Gascoynes die young,' he said again. In response to the words, his heart hammered in his chest, as if threatening to end him before he could walk down the aisle. He forced himself to ignore it, keeping his face neutral so as not to frighten his fiancée with his suffering.

She was just as silent, as she considered his words. Then she said, 'Thank you for making me aware of your plans in the matter. Much can happen between now and the end of our lives, however short or long that time may be. And I could not guarantee you children, even if you wanted them. That said, I see no reason why we cannot continue tomorrow and marry as we meant to do.'

What had he been expecting her to say? He analysed his own heart on the matter and could not decide if it was relief or dread he was feeling at the prospect of tomorrow's ceremony. But it was apparent that she was not going to cry off. And it did not really matter what he wanted. As a gentleman, it was too late for him to change his mind. 'Very well, then,' he said, at last. 'We will be married, just as we planned.'

'As we planned,' she agreed, with a slight smile that said his warnings had been useless. He suspected she had not believed a word of what he had said to her and still assumed their lives together would be normal. It would be left to bitter experience to teach her, just as it had him.

Robert was not sure what sort of wedding Emma Harris had imagined for herself, but the next day's ceremony could not have been it.

On speaking with her mother, it seemed that that woman had hoped for a grand ceremony at St George's in London.

He had made it clear, as gently as possible, that when one was orchestrating a quick wedding after a reputation-saving proposal, one did not call attention to the fact with pomp and ceremony. When reason seemed to have no effect, he reminded her that the London church was booked for months in advance and nuptials there would mean waiting until the social season was over.

The thought of delaying any benefits that the marriage might entail was enough to convince Mrs Harris of the need for a simple ceremony at the village church.

If the bride had an opinion, one way or the other, he did not know it. She had made it clear that she left the details of this arrangement to her parents. Perhaps she was as great a social climber as her mother appeared to be, but she was smart enough not to press for more than she could reasonably achieve.

Maybe she never spoke up for herself in the ordering of her own life and was timid by nature. Or perhaps it was the accident that had rendered her so docile. She had seemed sharp enough when he had spoken to her, last night. It would be just his luck if he had caused a problem far more severe than any slight to her reputation. No man wanted a wife that would argue each decision he made. But though they claimed to want a bride who was easily led, neither did they want one with diminished intellectual capacity. If he had ruined her chances at marrying another with that bump on the head, he owed her the protection of his name.

Whatever her problems, he was doing the right thing by marrying her. In exchange, her father would provide the money that would allow her to live in comfort and he would be able to recover from the debacle of the tin mine investment. He would not go as far as to call the end result of the accident fortuitous. But it was not as bad as it could have been, considering. They were both still alive. And, if he kept his distance from her after their marriage, she would remain so.

Today, she was there, waiting for him at the church, in a blue-silk gown with deep scallops of lace. A veil was hiding the yellowing bruise on her temple and she held a man's walking stick in one hand to ease the weight on her twisted ankle. Despite those accommodations, she was a pretty bride, albeit a tall one. He had got a sense of her height when she had come to meet him the previous evening, but he had never stood close beside her. As she turned to face him, she met his gaze with only the barest lift of her chin.

'Miss Harris,' he said, removing his hat and bowing.

'Sir Robert.' She made the mistake of attempting a curtsy, only to pitch forward as she tripped over her own feet.

Her mother let out a hiss of disapproval at her stumble, as though Emma was being deliberately annoying. He could see the girl readying an apology, even as she attempted to catch her balance.

Without thinking, Robert grabbed for her, stepping in to let her collapse against him instead of falling. It was surprisingly pleasant to feel the weight of her in his arms and, for a moment, he regretted that there was not some actual affection between them.

She looked at him with confused eyes which were both huge and a brilliant blue, then muttered, 'I am so sorry', as she tried to pull herself upright again.

'It is all right,' he assured her, adding a gentle smile so as not to alarm her further. 'Let us go and see the vicar, shall we?' Then he tucked the hand that was not clutching the stick into the crook of his arm and led her into the church.

As if he sensed that the circumstances for it were unusual, the vicar kept the ceremony short and did not waste his breath on a sermon about the responsibilities of the married couple. It was just as well, since Robert had no intention of obeying the biblical instructions to be fruitful.

When they came to the vows, the bride answered with only the slightest hesitation and he made sure his own voice was clear and decisive in response. Almost as quickly as it had begun, it was over and they had been pronounced man and wife.

Then the vicar led them to the side to sign the church register. He signed his name and stared down at the book as his wife, Emma, signed hers as well. The act should not have felt so strange. He had watched it happen, each step of the way. But now that the knot had been tied, he felt an answering tightness in his collar, as if all the air had been sucked from the room, and his heart began to pound again.

Not now.

He willed the feeling away, digging his nails into the palms of his cold hands, and focused his thoughts on the future until his body and mind were under control again.

Beside them, there was a faint clearing of a throat. His new in-laws had signed as witnesses. Harris was beside him, jabbing an elbow into his side. 'And I expect you'll be wanting this.' Then he reached into his pocket and produced a cheque, signing it with the same pen used to record their marriage, blotting it and handing it to Robert.

Perhaps he had not fully recovered his wits, because he reached for it automatically, even while his brain screamed that he must refuse. Before he could stop himself, he took the money, tucking it hurriedly into his jacket pocket as the vicar looked away in disgust.

He turned to look into the shocked eyes of his bride. Then, without saying a word, she tapped her stick on the ground and hobbled out of the church.

Chapter Four

She had never been so embarrassed in her life.

When this offer had come, some part of Emma had assumed that it might be possible to escape the worst of her parents' criticisms by marrying and leaving their house. But it seemed that life with Sir Robert Gascoyne would be more of the same. Could he not at least have pretended in the church that there was a reason other than money that had convinced him to take her?

'Lady Gascoyne!'

Now she had embarrassed herself by looking around the churchyard to see where that lady might be. As of today, she was Lady Gascoyne and she must learn to answer when called. She turned reluctantly to look at her husband. 'Yes?'

'The staff have prepared a wedding breakfast at our home.'

'Of course,' she said, wondering why he had bothered to pretend celebration over something that was clearly a matter of business to him.

'Now that we are married, you will be riding in my carriage,' he said in a tone of a mild reminder.

She was standing in front of her parents' equipage, ready to climb in. 'Of course,' she said again, taking the arm he offered and allowing him to lead her, like a child, back to the correct carriage. He was looking at her with concern, as if he was not sure she understood plain English.

It should not have surprised her that the godlike man she had managed to marry thought she was a fool. She was wandering in the churchyard as if she had forgotten why she'd come there. She gave a resigned sigh. 'I understand who I am and where I am to live.' Then she remembered that she was angry with him and added, 'I understand just as clearly as the vicar understands your reason for marrying me.'

He winced. Then he said, 'It is not too late for us to attempt discretion, in some things at least. Let us get into the carriage before we continue this discussion.'

He would have been more apt to say argument, for Emma did not feel like discussing anything. But in her experience, arguing was pointless since she always lost and was left feeling worse than she had when she'd begun. So, she took the arm he offered and let him help her into the carriage.

Now that they were alone inside it, there was another moment of awkward silence, which gave her far too much time to admire her new husband. Just as he had at the church, she was near to struck dumb by the perfection of him. He had held her when she stumbled and, during the vows, she had allowed herself to imagine that it was possible to make a proper match with him, despite the lack of children.

Then he had ruined it all.

As if sensing what she was thinking he spoke. 'It was not I that wrote the cheque, you know.'

'I know,' she said. 'I am used to such behaviour from my father and should not have been surprised by it. But I had hoped…' It had been unrealistic to expect him to care for her. But she had hoped he could be more subtle in revealing the truth.

'I should not have taken it while we were still in the church,' he said. 'But it happened so suddenly that I could not think of a good way to refuse.'

If she was honest, that described how she had come to be married to him. She had meant to say no. Yet here she was. 'I understand.'

Now they were on the same road where she had had her accident and, from there, they proceeded to the long drive with its impressive view of the great house that was Gascoyne Manor. Her mother was right. It was a beautiful edifice with two long wings of grey stone stretching out on opposite sides of the wide front door. The gardens outside were equally marvellous, with herb knots and a hedge maze that Emma looked forward to exploring.

When they reached the entrance, Sir Robert hopped out ahead of her to help her to the ground. But before they could make it to the front door, they were charged at by an enormous black dog. Recognising a newcomer, it threw itself at Emma, planting its front paws on her shoulders and giving her a sloppy kiss on the face.

'Theobald, no.' Robert grabbed the dog's collar and tugged him back to the ground. Then he turned to her, sheepish. 'He is untrained, but harmless.'

She thought of Sir Robert as he had looked on the first day she'd met him and thought that the description could just as easily have been turned towards him. He had been a good-looking beast, but clearly in need of a grooming.

Today? His hair was trimmed, his face clean-shaven and the buttons on his coat were both straight and shiny. Though he might have failed her in the matter of the settlement, he had made an effort in other ways.

'That is all right,' she assured him, turning back to the animal he held and patting it on the head. 'I like dogs. I have simply never seen one so large before.'

'He normally stays in the stables with the

horses,' her new husband replied. 'But you will find him an excellent companion on walks in the yard, should you choose to take them.'

'I will remember that,' she said, turning to greet her parents whose carriage was just arriving. Then, Sir Robert invited them into the house, leading them to the formal dining room where the celebration had been pre-pared.

If the wedding breakfast was any indication of the quality of the staff at Gascoyne Manor, then Emma had nothing to fear over manag-ing the household. The room was spotless and the table linens blindingly white. The cook had prepared heaping trays of smoked trout and shirred eggs, buns, fruit, champagne and a wedding cake dressed with candied fruit and fresh flowers.

But her mother ignored it all, most im-pressed by the silver engraved with the fam-ily crest. 'That is you, now, Em,' she said, toasting with an engraved glass and running her finger lightly along the G. 'That is you.'

Emma winced, glancing at her husband and hoping that he had not heard. 'That is my new name,' she admitted in a whisper. 'But I am still just as I was.'

'And yet you are also Lady Gascoyne,' her mother announced with a giggle. 'Can you imagine what fun you will have here? And what a lovely family you will raise?'

'Of course,' Emma lied, drinking deeply from her wine, so she need not answer further. If her husband had been serious in his pronouncement on the previous day, children were the last thing she needed to worry about. It was probably just as well. Thus far in life, she'd shown no signs of natural feminine ability. It was unlikely that those skills would blossom magically in time to make her an adequate mother to one child, much less a brood of them.

After that, Emma applied herself to the food on her plate and kept her mouth full, making it impossible to respond to the barrage of marital advice coming from her mother's side of the table. It was embarrassing that her parent felt the need to remind her of her duties in front of her new husband. But there was no getting a word in when her mother had decided to give her opinion and trying to make the harangue into a conversation would only prolong the agony.

When breakfast finally was over, they saw her parents off at the door. 'You will see us soon,' her mother reminded her. 'Then we will plan your social season.'

Emma cast a worried look at her husband. He did not quite frighten her. But it was clear to both of them that this was never the plan that either of them would have chosen. She doubted she had the nerve to begin throwing parties in his house without at least discussing the possibility of them. 'Allow us a few weeks to get to know each other, before you buy a new ballgown,' she said, colouring in embarrassment.

'Of course,' her mother agreed. 'Every happy couple deserves a honeymoon. We will leave you lovebirds alone for a month. But no longer.'

'I will write when it is time,' Emma replied, pushing her mother into the carriage and waving her off.

They watched in silence as her parents rode away from the manor and Emma could not but help thinking how strange it was to have left her family's home for the last time. At the thought, she felt both free and frightened. Her new husband would have his own expectations of her, but he could not possibly be as judgemental as her mother. Until she knew him better, she had no idea if he would take enough interest in her to bother with having any kind of opinion, good or bad. If he did not want her to be a mother to his children, what was her role here to be?

That thought left her feeling empty. She was equally confused as to what would happen, now that there was no reason to make polite conversation for the sake of her parents.

By the slightly puzzled look on her husband's face, he must be feeling the same. Then he announced, 'I think it is time to give you a tour of your new home.' Sir Robert gave a vague gesture to the surrounding walls, as if he were introducing her to a person rather than a place. 'You have been here before, of course, but you were in no condition to enjoy it.'

He walked her through the spaces she had only glanced at on her last hurried exit from the Gascoyne manor. It was everything that her mother had hoped for her. The public rooms were large, high-ceilinged and numerous. And her husband the recluse had not been using any of them.

'Do you enjoy this house?' she asked tentatively. 'It is quite a grand place for a single person to live in.'

'Single no more,' he reminded her with a tight smile. 'But no, if you must know. I do not enjoy it. It has been more a prison to me than a home.'

'Then why do you stay?' she asked.

'It is my family home,' he said blankly. 'There has always been a Gascoyne at the manor since my ancestor built it.'

It was not actually an answer, it was an excuse. But there was no point in telling him so.

What she could say was the truth. 'It is quite the loveliest house I have ever been in.' The windows in the drawing room were high and clear. The library had a stone fireplace carved in leaves and vines. And as expected, there was a ballroom, with its vaulted ceiling and musicians' gallery surrounded by white marble balustrades. Their pleasing design was marred only slightly by the dust on the floor and a garish and peeling fresco on a wall at the end of the room that reminded her how rarely it must be used.

She remembered her mother's command that she have a ball as soon as she was able. With the condition of the room, soon was later than her mother might expect. At the moment, it was the only space in the house showing too much disrepair to hold guests.

As if he could read her mind, her husband said, 'If you are contemplating a gathering here, you would do well to refrain from it. Gascoyne Manor is not open to guests.'

She looked back at him in surprise. She had known he was somewhat of a hermit before she had agreed to marry him, but it had not occurred to her that he might expect the same behaviour of her.

It was a conundrum. She had not really wanted to entertain at all. She was very much of a mind with Robert on the subject that it would be better to avoid company and save herself the inevitable embarrassment of a social faux pas. But now that it looked as if it might be forbidden, there was an irresistible appeal to it. 'Is there a reason for this prohibition?'

'The last ball was held by my grandfather to celebrate his youngest son's engagement. The couple were killed in a carriage accident before they could even marry.'

'That is very sad,' she agreed. 'And the house has been closed since?'

He shrugged. 'My first wife insisted on holding dinner parties and small gatherings. But something untoward always seemed to happen. At the last one, the fish was bad. The guests were sick for weeks after.'

'I see,' she said, trying not to think of the trout at breakfast. 'But a few minor problems in entertaining are normal. They do not make for a curse.'

'But problem on top of problem does,' he said. 'You were the first guest to cross the threshold in three years and look at the reason for it. I had to carry you in unconscious because of my own carelessness at the reins.'

'You blame yourself for the accident that brought me here?' she said, surprised.

'Who else would I blame?' he said, equally surprised.

'I was the one who fell in the ditch,' she said. 'As usual, I was not watching where I was going and tripped on a rabbit hole.'

'But I was there when it happened,' he said, as if that was explanation enough.

'And it was a good thing you were,' she agreed. 'If you had not been there to rescue me, I might still be lying in a heap beside the road.'

'Or you might be safe at home, unhurt,' he reminded her.

And unmarried. Neither of them said it, but the pause in the conversation was perfect to hold those words.

'Unhurt for the moment,' she completed. 'You do not know me well, but I am uncommonly clumsy, always tripping over my own feet and embarrassing myself. The most recent fall was just another example of my lack of grace. I am sorry that you think it was your fault.' And she sincerely hoped it was not the reason he had married her. She could accept that he had married her for her money and because of her father's bullying over lost honour. But marrying her out of obligation to some imaginary curse was beyond understanding. 'But I prefer to focus on the positive in the situation. You rescued me. That is all that matters.'

'I will accept your gratitude,' he said in a grudging tone. 'I hope the time never comes that you regret it.' As they had talked, he had led her up the main stairs. Now they stopped at a door in the wing of family bedrooms. 'And this is your room,' he said, opening it and gesturing to a well-appointed bedchamber.

'My room,' she repeated, staring into it and taking note of the connecting door that must lead to his adjoining bedroom. With so much space, it made no sense to share a room. But neither had she considered how large and intimidating the house would be and how lonely. If she admitted to being afraid of her own bedroom, her new husband would think she was a complete ninny. Probably even more so than he already did.

'You did not think I would house you in the stables,' he said, smiling at her confusion.

'It is just that my parents share a room,' she said.

'Is their home so small that they must?'

he asked. 'It did not appear to be so, when I was there.'

'Not overly so,' she replied. 'But they choose to share a room.'

'And we do not,' he reminded her. 'We had a discussion about it, yesterday.'

'You said that you did not want children,' she said, wishing that her voice did not sound so thin and needy.

There was a long and significant pause. 'I do not think you fully understood what I was trying to tell you.' He reached to take her hand as if reassuring a child. 'I do not know how much you know about the expectations between a husband and wife.' Now, he coloured, as if he feared he would need to explain what he was hinting at, in broad daylight and right outside the bedroom door.

'My mother taught me the proper running of a household and the management of servants. And…she explained other things as well,' she assured him. She had even explained several ways to prevent the chance of children when performing the marital act. Perhaps this was what her husband was afraid of having to explain. But he could not mean what she thought he was saying.

He let out a relieved breath. 'Then I expect you are nervous at the prospect of what is to come,' he said, clearing his throat.

'No more so than I have been for the last week,' she said, trying and failing to meet his gaze which was fixed on the floor.

'I wanted to let you know that you do not have to worry. As I explained last night, I have no intention of visiting you.'

He had said nothing of the kind on the previous evening. He had told her that he did not want children, but he had said nothing about leaving her chaste on her wedding night. 'It has been a very busy day,' she said, trying not to be disappointed at the unexpected frailty of the man she had married. 'We are both very tired.'

He shook his head, as if she had misunderstood again. 'I think, since we have very little in common, that it will not be necessary for me to visit you in that way on this night, or any other.'

He did not want to sleep with her. At all. Her mother had assured her that, once married, she would no longer have to worry about her deficiencies in appearance or deportment. Men were none too particular about the marital act and enjoyed it with any willing partner. But her husband's obvious distaste of her overcame his natural inclinations and he was disguising it in vague references to social compatibility.

Or perhaps she was to blame, as she always seemed to be. 'Familiarity can grow over time,' she insisted. Once she knew him better, perhaps she could find a way to transform herself into someone that he might desire.

'That is true,' he said, clearly surprised to find his decision questioned. 'But no matter how much time passes, there is no reason to believe that we will become quite that familiar.'

Was it truly so hopeless? She blurted the question she was afraid to have answered. 'Is there something about me you find offensive or off-putting?'

'No,' he said, almost too hurriedly to be believed.

'Is there some incapacity on your part?'

'Good God, no.' This denial came even faster.

'Then what is your reasoning?' she said, wishing he would simply be honest and tell her she was unattractive.

'It is simply that I have lost one wife and do not mean to lose another,' he snapped.

This stopped her. He had said very little about his last wife, hurrying her through the portrait gallery so fast she had got barely a glance at the painting of the woman that had hung beside his. Perhaps her loss had affected him more deeply than he liked to reveal and he needed time to settle the grief he still felt for her before taking another woman to his bed.

If he missed his first wife so much, then, why had he remarried at all? Then Emma remembered the money that had changed hands before the ink was even dry on the register.

But that still did not give him the right to cloak his feelings about her in lies. 'Despite the curse you keep going on about, there is no reason to think that I will not survive child-birth,' she replied. 'My mother has often told me I have the grace of a plough horse. I suspect I have the strength of one as well.'

'Do not speak of yourself in that way,' he snapped, then, as if realising how he must sound, his voice gentled. 'I do not care to hear what your mother thought of your deportment. I have no problem with it.' He reached out to take her hand, giving it a gentle squeeze as he spoke the next words. 'There is nothing wrong with you. But if you are married to me, there is every reason in the world to believe you are at risk. And that is why I have no intention of putting your health in danger by attempting an act that might start a family. It is better that we live as strangers than to court disaster.'

'I see.' In truth, she still did not. Now that she had finally managed to overcome her dazed infatuation enough to speak to him, it appeared that he meant to base their entire marriage on nonsense.

It did not matter what he claimed. Considering what her mother had always told her about her matrimonial chances, a lie made far more sense. He knew he had been trapped and now he was punishing her. But what good did it do to wonder about his reasoning if she could not manage to change his mind? How could she bear to live with him if she could not?

Then she remembered the best piece of advice her mother had given her in the final week of instruction in the womanly arts. Always agree with your husband—then, do as you wish.

She wished to have a normal marriage, just as her mother had. But that was a battle that could not be fought in a common hallway on their first day together. So, she swallowed her humiliation at his rejection and gave him what she hoped was a complacent smile. 'If you think that is for the best and you are my husband, then I must obey.' She turned to her room. 'I suppose I will acquaint myself with my new chamber, before it is time to dress for dinner,' she said.

'Dressing is not necessary, if you do not wish to,' he said, giving her a blank look. 'No one is here to see.'

'You are here,' she reminded him, trying to ignore the pang of loss over the fact that, since he did not want to think of her as a woman, he probably did not care what she did.

But she cared. She had a closet full of expensive and stylish dinner gowns, and she would not let them go to waste. Even if it did not matter to him what she wore, she must not let his disgust of her break her spirit. She was going to look her best. 'I assume that dinner is at eight,' she said, taking a deep breath and trying not to lose her nerve. 'You may wear what you like, but I will dress for dinner, as I usually do. Now, if you will excuse me?' She stepped into her new room, closed the door on her new husband and called for her maid.

Chapter Five

Damn it to hell.

This day was not going as he had hoped it might. First, there was the embarrassment over the settlement. Then his mother-in-law had behaved over breakfast just as he feared she would, as if the house now belonged to her, via her daughter.

He had at least thought that the matter of the bedroom had been settled yesterday, but it was clear that his bride had not understood him at all. She still held out hope that things could be normal between them.

She did not understand how difficult it would be for him, once they started on a path of intimacy, to walk the careful line that avoided completion of the act. It would be even more so with a woman who suited his tastes as she did. Even worse, her sudden surrender to his wishes probably meant she thought to wear him down on the subject of bedding her. It was a most unladylike reversal on her part. He was the one who should take the lead in matters of the bedroom. She was supposed to be the naive pupil, ready to accept his guidance.

Though she spoke as if she was unaware of her allure, when it came to matters of wardrobe, she was currently behaving just as any other woman of fashion might and choosing a gown that would display far more skin than a simple day dress might. She was going out of her way to be even more lovely than she already was, possibly meaning to tempt him.

He would not succumb to it. She could do as she liked, but that did not mean he had to respond to it. He would treat her costume as an ordinary part of the day, even if doing so meant he was going to have to dress for dinner.

His life was quite comfortable the way it was. It had not occurred to him, when marrying, that the details of it might change in any significant way. But with a woman in the house, he would not be able to keep to his usual habits of eating in day clothes by the sitting-room fire. Formality would be returning to his life, whether he liked it or not.

No matter her motives, he had denied her so much already he could hardly complain about something as small as this. Tonight, dinner would be at eight in the dining room, just as he should be accustomed to.

He rubbed a hand over his cheek, feeling the stubble forming there, and realised that there was no point in dressing without a shave. He surrendered and rang for his valet.

As he was shaved, he brooded on another matter that bothered him. There was also the annoying fact that he was quite sure she was not taking him seriously on the matter of the curse. There was something in the clear blue eyes looking back at him that was more than ordinary doubt. It was blatant scepticism.

He had not told her the whole truth, of course, nor had he told her father when they'd arranged the marriage. To share too many of the details about his family was to risk the Harris family coming to its collective senses and crying off. But she would change her mind about the curse soon enough, when she saw the effect it had on him.

But what if she didn't have to? Suppose he never had another incident?

The thought was so faint that he could barely believe he'd had it. He'd had no problems in months and had survived the wedding with no real problems. Was there a way to change the future by changing the course of his life with this new woman? She was as different from his departed Elizabeth as it was possible to be, tall and bright, to Beth's petite coolness. Hesitant where Beth had been sure. And of a totally different class than Robert, or his former wife.

She also insisted, above all things, that she was strong. Physically, perhaps she was. But today in the church, she had been meek and in need of reassurance. Perhaps her need for him had given him the strength he needed to survive his own problems. For all he knew, his entire life might have changed for the better, the instant he'd met her.

Or perhaps not. He had thought himself free many times before and had been wrong each time. There was no point in raising his hopes only to have them dashed again. For now, he must go on as he had been meaning to and keep his distance from her. Time would show him if there was any reason to change his mind or his plans.

She arrived at the dinner table at the appointed hour and took the seat that had been laid for her across the table from him. Though he'd meant to ignore her, he had to admit that it had been worth putting on a fresh cravat to see a woman so elegantly arrayed at his own dinner table. Her gown was of a white netting carefully embroidered along the sleeves and hem with verdigris leaves to match the green-velvet ones that had been used to dress her hair. The effect evoked a dryad that had fallen asleep under her tree and then rushed to table without brushing the fallen foliage from her curls.

But this presented a challenge. The gown she wore was cut low as he feared it would be and revealed a startling amount of bosom. He had been too polite to look when she had been injured and recovering in his house. But now he could not seem to pull his eyes away from the feast of soft curves arrayed before him.

He forced himself to look her in the eyes and smile, giving her a nod of welcome, but offering no compliments on her appearance.

The chilly expression he received in return proved that she had not yet forgiven him for his comments by the bedroom. If he truly had been so obtuse in his explanation that she had not understood him, he could see why she was angry with him. Now, it seemed there were multiple things being denied her and they were only on the first day of a lifetime together. He could only hope she would get used to her position in time and forgive him the restrictions.

Or perhaps he had annoyed her to the point of unsteadiness. As she reached for it, she came close to upsetting her wine glass. She saved it with a grab at the last second and left only a few red drops marring the perfection of the cloth.

For a moment, the elegant façade crumbled, revealing the unsure girl he had married. She looked as if she was bracing herself for censure. 'I am sorry,' she said, half to him and half to the servants.

What a strange idea. He had spilled more than his share of wine on this table and many others and had never considered it a serious error. It was certainly not the sort of thing that caused one to demur to the footman.

Robert looked at her, gave a half shrug of understanding and continued to eat.

'As I told you before, I am known for my carelessness,' she announced, as if some explanation was needed.

'Because of spilled wine,' he replied, confused.

'And falls into ditches, broken crockery, stumbles over the furniture...' she gave a wave of her hand that almost upset her glass again '...you will notice, given time.'

'Or you will grow into your height and learn to control it better.'

'Grow into my height,' she repeated.

'How old are you?' he asked, realising that he had not bothered to find out before marrying her.

'Twenty-one,' she replied.

'And I suspect you have come to your full stature in the last year or two.'

'I hope so,' she replied fervently. 'My modiste despairs each time I come back to her. My measurements are never the same and nothing is long enough.'

'It takes time to learn the boundaries of a changing body,' he said. 'Men are aware of this in ways that women are not, I think. In the meantime, you will find this will help.' He reached across the table and moved her wine glass a few inches to the left.

She reached for it without effort, then stared at it in amazement. 'My mother would not have approved a change in table setting,' she said, staring at the glass. 'She told me things were ordered for a reason and to put them back exactly where I found them, after use.'

'Your mother is not here,' he reminded her.

'That is true,' she said, her expression brightening for the first time since he had met her. She was lovely enough under normal circumstances, but when she made an effort to smile at him, he had to remind himself again of his plans to avoid her bed.

Then he received a reminder of just why it

was he had made the plan in the first place. The butler appeared in the dining room, his posture a strange combination of apology and urgency. 'I am sorry Sir Robert,' he said. 'But there is an emergency. A fire in the village.'

Robert tossed his napkin aside and rose from the table. 'Saddle my horse. And send a wagon as well. Gather the able-bodied servants.'

'What do you expect to do?' his new wife said, surprised that he was leaving.

'At times like this, we must all come to the aid of our neighbours,' he said. It was especially true when one felt at fault for whatever had happened. If the curse on his marriage had caused some sort of disaster, then it was a further reminder of why he must hold to his original plan.

It was her wedding night and she was alone.

After his declaration that this was to be a marriage in name only, she should not have been surprised. But she had not thought that he would find an excuse to leave the house as well. His reasoning was noble and she could hardly argue with it. All the same, she had thought she sensed a certain amount of relief in him as he had left the dining room, as though he was eager for an excuse to abandon her.

She had thought for a moment, during the meal, that he had been looking at her as a man should look at a woman he had married. He had admired her. He approved. And he had been so helpful as to suggest a slight rearrangement of her wine glasses to make life less difficult. This brief kindness had been enough to make her think he would relent on the artificial distance he meant to keep between them.

Then he had left.

On her way from the dining room to her bedroom, she passed through the portrait gallery, the room that Sir Robert rushed through in the earlier tour due to the sad stories attached to so many of the subjects. But Emma had come to see the one person who had barely been mentioned in the discussion of the curse thus far.

She found her in place of honour beside the portrait of Sir Robert, just where she belonged. The painting was of a china doll of a woman, short and blonde with rosy cheeks and slim arms. Delicate feet peeped from beneath the hem of her gown. Her slender neck was wrapped in pearls, fastened with a jet cameo that looked so heavy that it was a wonder she did not bend from the weight of it.

At the end of the hall, there was a mirror that gave the viewer the illusion that they, too, were part of the gallery. Emma turned and looked into it now, flinching from what she saw there. He had been kind enough about her awkwardness at dinner. But that was not a matter of attraction as she had wished it to be. It was simply courtesy.

There was a perfectly logical reason he did not want to sleep with her. One had only to look at this reflection to see that. After looking at the sort of woman he preferred, there could be no logical reason for him to marry Emma other than for money.

He might make up a ridiculous story about family curses, but it was only an attempt to spare her the truth. They did not suit in any way she might have hoped on first catching sight of him. If he wanted anyone, it would be another wife like the one he'd had.

Emma could not be further from that, if she had asked God to make her the opposite of the woman in the portrait. Too tall, graceless and sturdy, as her mother sometimes called her. She must learn to face the fact that she was simply not lovable.

Now, it was a relief that her new husband was nowhere in the house, for it would have been very embarrassing if he had caught her crying in a public room over something that no amount of tears could change. It was even better that her mother was not here to see, for she would have mocked Emma for her sentimental feelings and reminded her that it had taken a trick to get her any kind of marriage at all. It was unrealistic of her to have hoped for happiness as well.

The knowledge made the tears fall faster as did the realisation that, since she had dressed for dinner, she was stuck without a handkerchief and not even a sleeve to blot her cheeks. She looked around to make sure that there were no servants within sight and went to the nearest window so she could wipe her face upon the back of the curtains. Then, she leaned her face against the windowpanes, letting the night-cooled glass calm her flushed skin.

When she straightened, her crying had stopped and her mood was as calm as it had been at dinner. She must accept that things were as they were and make the best of them. Her husband did not want her as a woman. But he had been kind to her at dinner and that was more than she was used to.

The fact that he could not love her did not matter. He might come to rely on her in other ways. Perhaps she could be a helpmeet to him. With his reclusive ways and his belief that every bad thing that happened was a part of his destiny, she could not think of a man who needed more help than he did.

That settled the matter. She would grit her teeth, smile with those gritted teeth and apply herself to the situation. She would do good, just as the Lord wished for her to do. And she would change the life and mind of her new husband and put an end to the fears that held him imprisoned alone in his house.

Chapter Six

Robert had not slept at all that night, working on the bucket line at the fire until well past dawn. When he arrived home, he called for a hot bath to scrub the smoke from his skin and apologised to his valet for the ruination of his rarely worn dinner clothing.

Apologising. He was beginning to sound like Emma. The thought made him smile. He hoped that she'd had a pleasant night after he left her and not lain awake in a strange bed, waiting for him to come home.

But he suspected she had for, according to the servants, she slept late.

He did not see her until luncheon, in the dining room.

'I suppose you are wondering what called me away,' he said with a grim smile.

'All the servants knew was that it was a fire,' she said.

'It was the first manifestation of the curse that you do not believe in,' he replied, hoping that she did not want to delve too deeply into his reasoning. 'Not even a day after our marriage, the vicarage burned to the ground.'

'That is horrible,' she said. 'Was anyone hurt?'

'No. All escaped unharmed.'

She thought for a moment. 'Then that is good news and not bad.'

'A fire is good news?' he said with a doubtful raise of an eyebrow.

'No one was hurt,' she reminded him. 'And what caused the fire?'

'An improperly cleaned chimney,' he said.

'Carelessness on the part of the vicar's wife, then.'

'You could say that,' he said. She might say it, but he would not.

'If the building were smote by lightening from Zeus, I might see it as a curse,' she replied. 'Or if we had been anywhere near the site of the fire. As I remember it, we were married in the church and not the vicar's home.'

'They are side by side,' he reminded her.

'And the vicarage has, or had, a thatched roof,' she agreed. 'It is quite miraculous that the fire did not spread to the church.'

'Not a miracle,' he said with a frown. 'It was with the effort of many men, me included, throwing water on the flames for the better part of the night.'

'So, you admit that, when misfortune struck, it was possible to mitigate the effects of it,' she said. In a way, that had been the reason he had gone. Mitigation, and the fact that he could not have borne the consequences he might face, had he remained home while people needed his help.

'It must be a very weak curse, if you were able to thwart it so easily.'

'It did not feel particularly weak while I was working last night,' he said, annoyed.

'I am sure the vicar and his wife are grateful for your help,' she replied. 'I will write to my mother to offer them a place to live while their home is rebuilt. Soon, everything will be back to normal.'

'Until the next problem,' he said, not convinced. 'I usually avoid mixing with the neighbours to spare them misfortune.' And to spare himself as well. One could not be bothered by what one could not see.

'I am aware of that,' she said, pausing cautiously. 'And that is why I must ask you what I am to do with these.'

'With what?' he said, looking up to see the pile of letters she had placed in front of her on the table.

'Invitations,' she said. 'Are there any particular ones you wish me to accept or decline? You have told me nothing of your acquaintances thus far, but I assume you have some friends in the area, even if you do not visit them often.'

Did he? It had been so long since he had visited any of them that he assumed they had forgotten them. 'There is no one in particular,' he said at last. 'In fact, I am surprised that you are receiving mail at all, much less one day after our marriage. I have not received such a stack before.'

'Never?' she asked. 'Because I am quite

sure that, as a single man, you would have been in demand as a guest at any party.'

'I am well aware of that fact,' he said tartly. 'But as I did not intend to marry again, I avoided the sort of gatherings that people would wish me to attend only to be paired off with eligible females...'

'So, you ignored or refused all invitations you got until the neighbours stopped trying to contact you,' she concluded for him with a shake of her head.

'But why are they trying now?' he said, confused.

'I suspect that the vicar has told his flock that you were helping to save his house on your wedding night,' she supplied, with a flush of embarrassment. 'Now everyone is eager to get a look at the woman who has caught you.'

'The fact might have been mentioned,' he said uneasily. The vicar's wife had wept in gratitude at his help and announced the news loud enough for all to hear. He had thought nothing of it at the time, for it was not as if he had meant to keep his marriage a secret.

But the complications that the news might bring had not occurred to him.

'They are also wondering why you were so eager to leave me, on our first night,' she said with a sigh.

He wanted to reassure her, but could not. Of course, he had also assumed that an unconsummated marriage would be something that only the two of them would know. By going to aid with the fire, he'd given people a reason to gossip. He could not even lie and claim no one had noticed. The stack of mail in her hand was proof that they had.

'Your silence does me no good at all,' she said with another sigh. 'Which of these should I accept?' She gave the topmost invitation a poke with her finger, as if expecting it might come to life and snap at her.

'None of them,' he said suddenly, wishing that there had been more time for her to learn the risks of social interaction.

'I cannot simply ignore the post and hope it will stop coming,' she said gently. 'It is one thing for a widower to go through a period of seclusion. But it is quite another for a newly married man and his wife to hide in the house and ignore everyone.'

'Perhaps it is unreasonable of you to expect me to change,' he countered.

'Or perhaps it is unreasonable of you to make me a laughing stock.' Her mouth snapped shut as if she was stifling the rest of her response. Then she took a breath, as if composing herself before speaking. 'You came to me the night before we married and set conditions on our union. And I agreed to them.'

He nodded.

'Last night, it was clear that I did not fully understand them.'

'That is another matter entirely,' he replied.

'On the contrary,' she replied. 'I am still learning to adjust to the fact that my husband does not want my company. But now I must contend with the scrutiny of others on the subject.'

'That was never my intent,' he argued. But intent did not matter. Why had it not occurred to him that, in making her a Gascoyne, he might be doubling his troubles and not lessening them.

For a moment, her lip trembled as if she might be on the verge of tears. Then she took another breath and it stopped. When she spoke again, her voice was steady, almost businesslike. 'Can you explain your reasoning for refusing these offers, or is it merely habit?'

This was the point where he could explain the truth to her. But it was too much, too soon. So, he settled for a half-truth instead. 'I have always thought that it was for the best to avoid gatherings, so that I did not spoil them in some way.' Hopefully, she would never learn just how bad things might be.

'You are talking of the curse again,' she said in a tone that said she thought he was being a superstitious old woman.

In a way, he was. As she had said before, avoiding people had been his habit for so long he had difficulty citing an example that would prove his argument. 'Things do not go well, when I am around,' he said at last.

'If the curse is on you and your family, the effects on those around you need not be your primary concern. Unless it is your own health that you fear for.'

'Of course not,' he said, not wanting to look like a coward. 'Any bad fortune that falls on me will happen wherever I am.' He just did not like displaying his weakness to the world.

'Are you sure it is not that you are ashamed of me?' Now her voice was barely above a whisper. 'It is not as if I am eager to go about in public. I am sure the vicar has not already told everyone that you have married beneath you. But now that they know your contempt of me...' She was staring at the pile of mail again, her cheeks colouring in embarrassment.

'I do not feel contempt,' he insisted. But in the rest, she was right. He had made her an object of curiosity and, if something was not done to stem it, the gossip about her would grow rather than dying away.

'But how will I believe you if you will not be seen in public with me?' she asked. 'What harm will it do to accept a few of these invitations?' she countered, before he could come up with another excuse. Then she added, 'I will likely embarrass you in some way, for I am exceptionally graceless when I try to go about in society. But that is bound to happen, sooner or later. It might be easier if we just get it over with.'

She would embarrass him? 'That idea had never occurred to me,' he insisted. In fact, it was the least of his worries.

She brightened somewhat at the reassurance. 'Lady Weatherby is holding a musicale in three nights' time. The greatest risk to anyone at such events is a flat soprano. You need fear nothing from the curse and I will try not to disgrace us with my awkwardness. It will likely be a thoroughly dull evening and exactly the sort of thing we need for our first appearance as man and wife.'

Just the thought of going out in public made his throat tighten. But perhaps it had been so long since he'd tried that he had forgotten how dull things might be. Just the thought of attending a concert in a country drawing room made him want to doze in his chair. What could go wrong? He had managed the wedding without difficulty and the firefighting as well. Perhaps his troubles were over.

Then he looked at his new wife who was staring at him, part in hope, part in dread of this latest refusal. He had denied the poor woman everything she should have expected from a normal husband. How could he say no again? 'Very well,' he said, giving up. 'Accept the one invitation. But do not blame yourself if it all goes terribly wrong.'

Chapter Seven

After the conversation at lunch, Emma was left wishing that her mother had taken more time to research more than titles and property. Surely there should have been a note that Sir Robert Gascoyne's reclusiveness was a sign that, though he seemed so perfect when she looked at him, he was mad as a March hare.

The idea of remaining childless had been shocking enough. But she had thought it the most extreme thing she would hear from him. Now, it seemed that there might be an endless list of conditions on their interactions that she might not yet be aware of.

It was some consolation that she had got him to yield on attending the Weatherby gathering. It was a sign that change might be possible. She just had to make sure that the event went well, to convince him that there was nothing to fear from accepting further invitations.

Of course, that plan had its own problems attached to it. To accomplish it, all she had to do was develop grace and poise that she'd not had at any previous point in her life. It had been kind of Sir Robert to suggest at dinner that she would grow more co-ordinated with time. But this miracle of maturity was not likely to arrive in time to save her first appearance as Lady Gascoyne.

When some social failure on her part occurred, which it was surely likely to, he would blame it on his curse and use it as an excuse to keep them both home in the future. If she truly wished to help her new husband, then she must begin by proving to him that the world would not end if they left the house. She would simply have to be on her best behaviour to make sure the musicale was without incident.

It was something to ponder during a largely empty afternoon. Her husband had worked himself to exhaustion the night before and was probably enjoying a well-earned nap. But

Emma had no idea how she was expected to fill her own time. The menus for the week had been approved. It was too late in the day to make calls, even if she knew someone other than her mother that wanted visiting.

It had taken no time at all to write to that woman and encourage her to reach out to the vicar and his family. But she took care not to invite her mother to the house. If she was honest, having a day without her mother's criticism had been surprisingly liberating.

But now that she had this freedom and no one was trying to organise each minute of her day with ladylike education, what was she to do with her time?

She looked out the window to see the dog that had greeted them on the previous day staring longingly back at her from the yard. Sir Robert had suggested that she exercise him and herself. Perhaps now was the time to do it.

She opened the French doors to the morning room and he approached, sitting just outside and making no effort to pass over the threshold, but wagging his tail encouragingly from the other side.

'Are you lonely?' she asked.

This elicited a puzzled canine frown and another thump of the great tail, as if to say he did not understand her, but was happy to agree with anything as long as he could hold her attention.

'Well, I am,' she answered for him. 'And I think we could keep each other company on a walk through the yard. What say you to that?'

The dog stood, shifting eagerly from foot to foot, and then ran a little way away, looking back as if urging her to follow.

'Who am I to argue with such a polite gentleman?' she said, taking off after the dog. For a time, they rambled through the kitchen garden and he scared the rabbits out of the lettuce. Then they wound down the hill towards the stables and past, into the open fields beyond the formal grounds.

It was a beautiful day to be out of doors, watching sleepy bees and butterflies drinking from the wild flowers in a meadow. Perhaps, next time, she might bring her sketchbook. If this was her future, maybe it would not be so bad to be mistress of Gascoyne Manor.

But, apparently, the dog had other ideas

of what made for a perfect afternoon walk. Before she could stop him, he had darted through a gap in a fence and was running free in the nearby pasture.

'Theo, come back here. Come!' she shouted, then muttered, 'You stupid animal', under her breath as she climbed the stile to start after him. It would be just like her to lose her husband's favourite dog in the first week of their marriage. She suspected that would be far harder to forgive than a little spilled wine at dinner.

The huge dog cast a long look over his shoulder at her, pausing for a second as if he meant to obey. Then he started forward again, clearly on the scent of something more interesting.

'There are rabbits much closer to home, you horrible beast,' she shouted after him, stumbling over a tussock.

Then she saw what it was that the deranged dog had decided to chase. He was less than one hundred yards away from her, standing at the feet of a full-grown bull, barking up into the wide, angry face and wagging his tail as if it was the best joke in the world to risk his life in such a way.

Emma froze, momentarily at a loss for what to do. She was not a proper country girl, having spent most of her life in the confines of London where there was nothing more dangerous to be found than the occasional tomcat. But even she was aware that the last place she should be was near the behemoth that was facing down Theo. It did not matter if her husband was angry about the fate of the dog. He would doubtless be even more angry to send for a surgeon if she was gored half to death on the first full day of their marriage.

She began backing away, slowly. In her mind, she heard her mother's words that a lady must never seem hurried in any of her actions. Her job was to float, serene, from one place to the next.

Emma had never been particularly good at it. She was even worse when trying to do it backwards, so as to keep an eye on the bull. It did not appear that he had noticed her yet. But he certainly would if she tripped over her own feet trying to walk in reverse.

So, slowly, she turned, faced the direction

she had come from and hurried, in the most ladylike manner possible, away from the bull. But hurrying did not seem fast enough, so she bustled.

Then he saw her. At least she assumed that was what had happened. From behind her, she heard a bellow of rage and the sound of gathering hoof beats, rapidly closing.

It was then that she threw all maternal advice aside, hoisted her skirts and ran. When she reached the fence, she did not bother with the stile, but put a hand on the top and hurdled over it, her heels barely clearing the rail, hitting the other side still at a dead run. Now she heard the bull behind, reaching the fence, snorting and angrily pawing at the ground, unable to follow.

And the foolish dog that had got her into trouble was dancing around her feet, grinning and wagging as if they'd had the most wonderful walk ever.

From the hillside near the house, she heard a whoop of what sounded like mirth, and saw her normally stern husband pelting down the hill to stop at her side as well. 'Emma!'

Perhaps it was not the first time he had used

her name. But she had never heard it done with such emotion before. 'I am sorry,' she said, automatically.

'Magnificent!' he said, between pants of exertion as he arrived at her side.

'What is?' she asked, looking around her.

'I have never seen a woman run like that,' he supplied, grinning at her.

'I am sorry,' she said, again.

'Do not be so. I suspect most women would at least attempt it, given the provocation you had. Few would be as successful as to vault a fence,' he said, sounding strangely proud.

'I have not given the matter much thought,' she said, 'And I am not sure I could do it again, even if I tried.'

'Your ankle,' he said with a nod of remembrance at her previous injury. 'How is it feeling?'

'Much better, thank you,' she said, surprised that it had not given her the least bit of trouble during her escape.

'Perhaps, for your next feat, you might try something more sedate,' he said. 'Like walking in locations of the property that are not bullpens. And before you apologise, that is my fault, not yours. I suggested you walk the dog and should have known that he would lead you there. For some reason, he is great friends with Hercules and the bull tolerates him.'

'Hercules,' she said, staring back into the pasture.

'It was the name he had been given, when I bought him,' Sir Robert replied, staring back in the direction of the bull. 'I have called him many things since, some not nearly so polite.'

'And if you do not like him why, exactly, did you buy him?' she said.

He was giving her a look that said the answer to this question should be obvious. She blushed as he explained.

'There are many farms in the area that have at least one cow on them. But if milk is wanted, or veal, the assistance of the male of the species is required at some point.' He gave her another pointed look, to make sure she required no further details.

Her blush deepened.

'My goal was to hire his services to the local farmers. But, due to the luck of the Gascoynes, a plan that should be as simple as letting nature take its course failed utterly.'

'In what way?' she said, surprised.

'When presented with his sole purpose in life, Hercules was…uninterested.'

'He did not…?'

'Did not and would not,' Sir Robert said, shaking his head.

'Then why do you keep him?' she asked, staring at the bull in astonishment.

'Knowing what I do, I cannot sell him,' he replied. 'Who would want a bull that refuses to perform his only duty? And, while you might think it sensible to turn him into table fare, I could not bring myself to eat him. Especially knowing the price I paid for the roast.'

'How very strange,' she said.

'He is still as bad-tempered as others of his ilk, though, and I recommend you give him a wide birth. If you take Theo out, walk him on a lead. If you do not, do not bother to chase him, should he bolt. I have taught him a number of tricks, but the one that eludes him is answering to his name when called.' Then he shrugged and said, 'Do not worry about him. He never comes to harm and will return home when he is ready.'

'Yes, Sir Robert,' she said, resisting the urge to curtsy. Between the shock of confronting the bull and the admiring look on her husband's face, it was not her ankles that were feeling weak, it was her knees.

'Robert is sufficient, Emma,' he said, his smile returning. 'There is no reason to be so formal, when we are at home together.'

His voice was gentle, as it had been in the church when he'd said his vows, and she could not help staring up at his face, rendered as speechless as she had been the first time she'd seen him. She had forgotten how very green his eyes were. But a warm green, if that was even possible, as if there was a flame burning somewhere in the depths that had not been there before. Was it because of her? For his expression seemed to say that, though he might have looked at her before this moment, he had never really seen her as he was seeing her now.

She looked down at her feet, not wanting to notice the moment when the light in his eyes dimmed and everything returned to normal.

'Very well, Robert,' she replied and felt her cheeks grow pink as she repeated his name.

He held out his arm to her, nudging her elbow to regain her attention. 'And now, perhaps I can escort you back to the safety of the house.'

It was probably no more than a courteous gesture. But a sidelong glance at his face revealed a smile that was like a shared secret between them and she accepted both it and his proffered arm. 'Thank you, Robert. I would like that very much.'

Chapter Eight

The woman sitting across the table from him at dinner that night showed no signs of the misadventure of the afternoon. She was not precisely poised, for she still had the uneasy look of one unaccustomed to her new position. But there was nothing about the smooth hair or satin gown to remind him that she had been running for her life only a few hours ago.

Yet he could not get the image of it from his mind.

When he had looked from the window of his study and seen her chasing butterflies with the dog, there had been a childlike innocence to her that he had not noticed in other women of his set. It had certainly been absent in his late wife Elizabeth, who was not given to flights of fancy, day or night.

It had occurred to him that he could leave his work, which was nothing more than another letter enquiring after his defunct mine, to join her in an afternoon of idleness. He had shown her the house on the previous day, but there was much about the grounds that she did not yet know.

As he had walked through the house to the door, he'd lost sight of her for a few minutes and wandered the grounds himself, unsure of which direction she might have taken. It was then that he'd remembered her companion and begun to worry. Theo the dog, when left to his own choices, always ended up in the one place on the property that was unsafe for the new mistress.

For a moment he could picture in his mind what would happen next, the fulfilment of the death curse not at some distant, preventable date, but right here and now, before his eyes. He was to be punished for the audacity of his plan by seeing an innocent woman bloody and broken, worse than she had been on the first day of their meeting. This time she would be unmendable.

As he had run towards her, it had seemed

as if the distance stretched ahead of him to miles. His breath laboured and his vision clouded at the edges, leaving a narrow tunnel showing only her, unreachable and far too close to disaster.

Then, she had recognised the danger before he could even bring himself to call out to her and lifted her skirts to bolt. When presented with the obstacle of a fence, she had leapt over it like a doe, not even breaking stride as she had come down on the other side. The sight of it had shocked him back to himself and he was able to release his held breath in a laugh of joy.

As he had run the rest of the way to meet her, he noted several things. First, his wife might be careless in ignorance, but she was no coward. Secondly, she could run like no one he had ever seen before. He could remember jumping fences with his friends as a schoolboy and the pathetic hurdles that some of them had managed, trying to outdo the prowess of their peers. But she had been magnificent, as graceful as a dancer.

Most interesting of all, his wife had fine legs and he had seen all of them. She had hoisted her skirts well past the point of decency, above where they'd hidden her garters. And she'd revealed thin ankles, well-turned calves and firm, long thighs. And had it been his imagination, or had he got a brief glimpse of…?

He took a long drink of wine, trying to unimagine what he was quite sure he had seen. It was even harder to do with her sitting in front of him in another dangerously low-cut gown, piling temptation upon temptation.

Noting his empty glass, she pushed the carafe in his direction and it tipped dangerously, spilling a few drops on the cloth before the footman could grab for it.

As the servant refilled his glass, she whispered an apology for her mistake and stared, embarrassed, down at her plate. It seemed that their talk of the previous evening had not fully freed her from the feeling that minor mistakes were unforgivable sins. It made him wonder just how difficult it had been to live in her parents' house, under continuous scrutiny.

But beyond her muttered apologies, and his insistence that they were not necessary, it seemed they had little to say to each other. Of all the things he had considered, when he had agreed to marriage, he had not expected to be bothered by quiet. Since he lived alone and was not in the habit of talking to himself, silence had been his old friend for some time now. But another person in the room seemed to create a void that had to be filled.

'Tell me about your family,' she blurted. The words seemed unusually loud in the space between them.

The sound of her voice was enough to startle him. But of all the topics she had to choose, why must it be that one? He set down his fork and gave her a pointed look that said some things were not appropriate for the dining room.

She ignored it and continued. 'Since they are my family now, it only makes sense that you tell me about them. I should hate to run into someone on the street who claims an acquaintance, only to embarrass myself with ignorance.' She was giving him what she probably hoped was an encouraging smile.

He did his best not to be moved by it and failed. At last, he surrendered and said, 'If you have heard of Major John Gascoyne, you know the extent of my family.'

'He is your brother,' she supplied, waiting for more information.

'My half-brother,' Robert said grudgingly. 'And only living relative. As I explained to you before, women do not survive in this family. Jack is the son of my father's second wife.'

'Jack,' she said, noting the familiarity. 'And I suppose the two of you were close, growing up.'

There had been a time they were, but that was before their grandfather had intervened and it was so long ago he could hardly remember it. He gave her another quelling look. When it was clear that she was not impressed by it, he said, 'No. Jack was deemed frail, and brought to live here. I was sent away to school and lived predominantly in London until Grandfather died and I inherited this house.'

'Clearly your brother has recovered from any infirmity,' she remarked. 'I hear his service at Waterloo was most impressive.'

At this, Robert grunted. He still remembered the sleepless nights he had spent while Jack was risking his life in service of the Crown and the nightmares of carnage that had left him shaking in puddles of cold sweat. 'He is lucky to be alive. He has always taken unnecessary risks and scraped through by the skin of his teeth. The military was just the sort of career that would attract him.'

Yet, when he had returned, there was no sign that it had made him a happy man. In their brief interactions since his service, the foolishly optimistic young man who had enlisted had returned as cold and brittle as Robert sometimes felt.

'Since he is alive and well, you admit that the supposed curse does not extend to all members of the family,' his wife prodded.

'The further he stays away from me, the safer he has been.' And the harder it had been for Robert to function.

'You deemed him safer in Belgium than in your own house. A very convenient curse, that has such conditions on it,' she said, her gaze unwavering as it met his.

But somehow it seemed to be true. He thought of their childhood together and how miserable it had been. Since that time, Jack had seemed to flourish, just as he had failed. Was there only enough happiness for one of them? Or had he kept his brother safe by suffering enough fear for both of them while waiting for Jack's return? 'It is what it is,' he said with a shrug and looked away, putting those feelings behind him.

'That is no answer,' she replied.

And now this stranger he had married insisted on probing at things he did not want to discuss. 'It is the only one I can give you,' he said, daring her to argue.

'Then you cannot expect me to put any faith in the accuracy of your beliefs,' she said, poking holes in his vague explanation, just as she poked the fish on her plate with her fork.

'That is because you have not had to live through the results of this curse, or whatever it is,' he replied.

'There is no evidence that I will, even now that I am here,' she said. 'I have always been in good health. As far as I know, my father continues to be successful despite his association with you. In fact, you have done him good by taking his unmarriageable daughter off his hands.'

'You were not beyond marriage when I met you,' he reminded her. 'You were still young enough to make a better match.'

'And yet I had not. Thus far, you were my only prospect.' She stared down into her wine. 'And even that has not been quite as I expected marriage would be.' She gave him another direct look, to remind him of her dissatisfaction with the direction her life had taken.

'You agreed to my main condition before we married,' he said. 'Do not complain now that it is too late to change your mind.'

She blinked in surprise. 'On the contrary, I have been told that an unconsummated marriage is reason for an annulment.'

'You are incorrect,' he snapped. 'And I will not be seeking an annulment, no matter what happens between us, nor should you. I gave my word in church that we would be together and I will not go back on it.'

'You also gave your word that you would love me,' she reminded him.

'And you assured me you were not expecting a love match,' he replied.

'I did not expect it of you. But it shows me what your word is worth that you could make the vow so lightly, knowing what your plans were.'

Love. He had said the word, of course. But she could hardly fault him for his interpretation of that line of the vows. Since marriages were arranged to secure property, wealth and honour, no one of his set took that particular part of the ceremony seriously. He had certainly never discussed emotion with his late wife, before or during their marriage. Yet he had missed her sorely when she was gone.

'I mean to care for you to the best of my abilities,' he said, at last. 'But I cannot do more than that. In the end, you may decide if it constitutes love or some inferior emotion. But do not think that you can argue me into doing more or take back the actions of yesterday and be free again. We are bound to each other permanently, no matter what you do or do not do.'

At the rebuke, her eyes went wide with surprise. Then she looked down hurriedly at her plate and muttered, 'I am so sorry. I had not intended…' The words trailed away to nothing as she returned to her meal.

He had won her obedience. But strangely, it left him feeling worse than her defiance had done. They ate the rest of the meal in a silence that had lost all comfort for him.

She should not have challenged him.

She had meant to make polite conversation and learn a bit about his brother, who lived only a few miles away and yet had not attended their wedding. Instead, she had quizzed him until the conversation devolved into an argument.

Just yesterday, she had vowed to obey him and planned, despite his indifference towards her, to be his helpmeet. Instead, she had questioned the odd parameters of his curse and hinted that she wanted to escape their marriage after only a day. She had regretted the words, even as she'd spoken them. They sounded as if she'd given up before she'd even tried to make things work between them.

It was some consolation that he had refused her. In any other man, Emma might have been pleased with firm commitment to a lifelong marriage. But from Robert, it was nothing more than confusing. This afternoon, he'd looked at her as if he might be developing some feelings for her. But tonight, he seemed to think that the bond of matrimony could exist outside of both love and carnality, rather like a business contract.

Her father might have approved this sort of level-headed sense in his daughter's spouse. But when it came to his own marriage, he worshiped the ground that her mother trod upon and she was equally in love with him. After seeing a union such as theirs, Emma had found her own to be disappointing in the extreme.

But she should not have mentioned annulment.

She vowed to cause no more trouble for the rest of the evening, even if it meant that she did not speak at all. When Robert suggested that they retire to the sitting room for the rest of the night, she followed meekly, ready to pass the time quietly, doing nothing that might offend.

The room was arranged with seating around

the fire and it was clear from the way he dropped into the wing chair on the left that it was Robert's habitual resting place to spend the time between dinner and bed. But as he picked up the book that lay waiting on the table beside it, he gave no indication as to where she was to sit. Apparently, she was to be left to make her own decision on the matter.

On the other side of the fire, there was a dainty sofa that seemed perfect for a lady, or, more accurately, the lady of the house. It was as if the room itself had made the choice for her. She belonged sitting opposite him, as the second half of a pair.

But she could not sit empty-handed for hours and do nothing. There were likely some interesting books in the library, but she had not bothered to choose any of them and did not want to call attention to herself by leaving the room so soon.

If she could find a bit of string, she might amuse herself with a solo game of cat's cradle, since she doubted her serious husband would be interested in children's games. But as of yet, her mending basket was totally empty. It was just as well, for she might have felt obligated to do handwork and she had no desire for that.

A brief circuit of the room revealed a handsomely carved chess set. Since Robert was still sitting in stony silence, there was no indication that he would want to play with her. But there was also a deck of cards, suitable for patience, a game that more accurately described what her life might be like from this time forward.

She settled herself carefully into the ladylike chair again, feeling just as uncomfortable as she had on the previous evening when she had retired alone. At least then her bed had been large enough to hold her. The dainty bench she was currently occupying was too shallow to do more than perch on the edge while waiting for the hours to pass.

She pulled the side table forward to lay out her game of cards and the unavoidable screech of the legs on the wood floor made her husband look up from his book in surprise.

She gave a nod of apology and pushed it back with an equally loud shriek. Then, she turned to the side and leaned forward, over the arm of the chair, shuffling the cards to lay out a tableau.

The seat gave an unsteady rock with her movement. Perhaps patience was too violent an activity for this side of the room. She stared into the fire for a moment, listening to the creak of the chair beneath her and trying to choose a more sedate activity.

A house of cards, perhaps. The movements involved would be slow and deliberate, and not the least bit upsetting to husband or furniture. She began her tower carefully, settling into a rhythm of balancing cards, hardly daring to breathe for fear of upsetting something or someone. It was going well. She had built three levels tall and was just placing the last card before starting a fourth when the house collapsed, the sound barely audible in the silent room.

But even that was enough to startle her and she leaned back suddenly as it fell, bumping the arm of her seat with her hip. With a shriek of strained joints, the sofa gave way entirely, collapsing out from under her. For a moment, she sat on the floor, in the rubble, unsure of whether to laugh or cry at her latest utter failure to be a proper lady.

Before she could struggle to her feet, Robert was there, his hand outstretched to take hers and pull her up, as easily as if she was a woman half her size.

'I am sorry,' she said, automatically.

'You have nothing to be sorry for,' he said, just as quickly. 'Why did you choose that particular seat?'

'I assumed it was mine,' she said, gesturing at the arrangement of the room.

'Actually, I keep it there for the cat that sometimes joins me, of an evening,' he said, trying not to smile. 'I had no idea it was so flimsy or I'd have replaced it long ago.'

'I sat in the cat's chair,' she said. 'I thought...' She did not want to mention what she'd truly thought, which was that she was occupying a dead woman's seat and it had rejected her, just as her husband had.

'Despite what it may look like, I am not going out of my way to make your life difficult,' he said with a gentle smile, 'but the least I can do to prove it is to find you a comfortable chair.' He glanced around the room.

'Let us see if there is something that suits you better.' Then he stood and offered her his wing chair.

'No,' she said hurriedly. 'I couldn't.'

'You can't sit down,' he said, pretending to be puzzled. 'Is there something wrong with your knees?'

'I can't sit in your chair,' she said, shaking her head at him, confused that he could not see the obvious.

'They are all my chairs,' he pointed out.

'Even the one I broke,' she said, embarrassed again.

'Even the one that collapsed under you,' he corrected. 'You did not throw it against the wall. The damage was not a malicious act, was it?'

'No. But it was my fault, all the same.' She was simply too large for a normal chair.

'You might just as easily have said that it was my fault for leaving such a rickety thing where anyone might risk themselves in using it. You are not hurt, are you?' he added, as if remembering that it was his obligation to see to her safety.

'Of course not,' she said, smoothing her skirt.

'Then, as you keep claiming, you are very resilient,' he said with another smile. 'Now, as to the location of your future seating.' He grabbed her by the arms, turned her and pushed her gently into the wing chair.

She landed on the cushion with a surprised sigh.

'Comfortable?' he asked.

'It is still warm,' she whispered, a little shocked by the heat of his body still lingering in the upholstery.

'But do you like it?' he asked. 'And do not think to lie to me for I will watch you and know the truth.'

She nodded. 'It is very comfortable.'

'Then from now on, it is your chair,' he replied, then removed the rubble that had been the seat she had destroyed. He glanced around the room. 'And I shall take this.' He walked to the window, where an even larger chair was arranged next to a small table and dragged the chair back towards the fire. 'Unless you prefer the light from the fire on your right. We can just as easily switch sides.'

'It is kind of you to offer, Robert,' she said. 'But this has been your sitting room longer than it has mine. You have already yielded your chair to me. I will not ask you to change position as well.'

'As you wish,' he said with a grin. Then he arranged the furniture accordingly so that he was in his usual place and his old chair took the place of her ruined one.

They sat in comfort for the rest of the evening and, as the mantel clock struck midnight, he rose with a yawn and proclaimed that it was time for bed.

She froze in her seat, unsure what was to happen next. There was no rule that she should retire when he did. Perhaps, since he did not want to visit her, it would be appropriate to wait a few moments before following him. Or perhaps she was expected to go first.

'May I escort you to your room?' he said, clarifying the situation for her.

She rose and let him take her arm and lead her up the stairs. When they arrived at her room, he released her and turned to walk down the hall. Then, as if in afterthought, he turned back. 'I am sorry for my shortness with you at dinner. It cannot be easy for you to put up with requirements that seem arbitrary. But they are the rules I have been living by, for some time now. I did not realise how difficult they had become. Goodnight, Emma.' Then, without warning, he leaned in, kissing her lightly on the lips.

He probably intended it to be a simple salute between friends, over as quickly as it was begun. But once their lips met, neither of them wanted to draw away. The touch was sweet and gentle, but they lingered over it, neither one wanting to be the first to see it end. When he finally raised his head, it was to look back at her with a dazed smile. 'Sleep well,' he muttered, then turned and hurried down the hall to his room.

'And you, Robert,' she said, breathless with surprise.

He had kissed her. It was the smallest possible kiss of apology, barely a brush of his lips against hers. All the same, it was everything she had dreamed her first kiss might be. And it had come on the second day of their supposed celibacy. Was he already weakening, or was it the sort of gesture he was accustomed to give his last wife as they settled for the night? The idea that it might have been a kiss intended for another was more than a little disappointing.

But before he had turned away, she had seen the look in his eyes and his smile of pleased surprise. He had enjoyed it and so had she. And she would lay in bed tonight, hoping that it was the first kiss of many.

Chapter Nine

After all intentions of keeping his distance, he had kissed her goodnight.

She must have been more upset by their dinner argument than she had revealed for as she had sat by the fire with him she had barely dared to breathe in his presence. And as it had been at dinner, the silence, which had been his constant companion for years, had worn on his nerves.

She had been trying too hard to please him, to make up for her earlier difficulty. In doing so, she had tried to force herself into a place she would not fit. Worse yet, he had allowed her to do it, not even noticing how uncomfortable she must be.

It was just one more example of how difficult the world could be when one was not the average size.

But it was clear that she took such things as personal flaws in her character. He had been careless not to notice the problem before it had happened and spare her from embarrassment. He'd have never thought to take such a chair for fear that exactly what had happened to her would happen to him. But he had forced her into a mould created for another and allowed her discomfort. If he meant to care for her, he must do better.

She needed reassurance that he would not always be so heedless and that their marriage would not always be as difficult as these first few days. So, he had kissed her. It was a harmless enough act and had seemed so natural at the time that he had done it without thinking.

And it had been as delicious as taking a single bite of a summer peach. It had left him wanting more. Now, Robert stared up at the canopy over his bed, baffled by the sudden wakefulness that the simple act had raised in him.

Normally, he slept deep and well, and, if he was honest, too often. With a lack of company, the days sometimes seemed to pass in a haze of unused time, books that did not hold his attention and nights that ended far too early. Now, he had a wife and things would be different. He'd made no real plan to change anything, but as he lay there, he could not seem to shake the feeling that the house was fuller. The air had a different quality, like a faint perfume.

Then he realised what it was. Perhaps he was imagining it, but he thought he could hear the sound of her through the bedroom door.

It was not snoring, nor could he complain that it was loud enough to be annoying. Simply the faint inhale and exhale of another person in the vicinity and the shift of the covers as she turned in her sleep. It was surprisingly comforting to know that there was another soul present where there had not been before. Without realising it had happened, he was smiling into the dark, a faint anticipation creeping into his soul.

But what, exactly, was he waiting for? There was not going to be a rustle of bed-clothes thrown aside and no soft steps on the rug as she came to the adjoining door.

He doubted that she had the daring, even though she was a strangely forthright girl on the subject of what she had expected in marriage. She might be sound asleep right now, dreaming whatever dreams she might have. Or she might be laying there, listening to him breathe and wondering the same things he did.

Considering the conditions he had set upon their marriage, all such thoughts were dangerous. The pair of them awake might lead to another wayward kiss in the dark, a touch to a caress, and caresses to greater prolonged intimacy. If he brooded on the presence of a woman so close in the darkest, loneliest hours of his life, his resolve would falter.

Consideration led to compromise led to action and eventual regret.

He thought of his last wife to cool his blood. It had been a fair marriage, all things considered. She had been a delicate creature, with wide blue eyes and a frame so small that, at first, he had been afraid that he might break her with a touch. But she had been accommodating in the bedroom and he had been cavalier when remembering his grandfather's warnings of a family curse. His own troubles had stopped while they were together. His luck and health were good, and his nerves were steady. When things were going well, his grandfather's warnings had sounded like nonsense.

Yet, a year later, he had been a broken man, digging graves.

He would not risk that again. He turned his head towards the neighbouring bedroom and blew a kiss to the woman sleeping there. Then, he turned deliberately away and thought of other things until sleep came.

The next morning, however, he was almost overcome with a desire to see her at breakfast. Perhaps it was not her company specifically that he missed, but simply the society of another human soul. Even though their conversations so far had often been unpleasant, they were still more welcome than sitting in silence by himself.

That had to be it. Being too long alone had left him susceptible to her in ways that went far beyond the carnal urges he had expected would be easily conquered. His need for companionship gave her an unexpected power over him and he was not sure he liked it.

Perhaps he should limit their interactions until he was confident that he could control himself, just as he had planned to do when he'd agreed to wed her. So, he ate breakfast in his room and took the morning post in his study, with the door closed against intrusion.

Even so, he could not get her out of his mind. In the bedroom, he listened for sounds of her in the adjoining room. In the study, he caught himself staring at the door, trying to imagine where in the house she might be. And when he tried to think of nothing at all, he remembered the sight of her uncovered legs as she ran from the bull.

When he had made the plan, he had not thought his unspent sexual energies would be aroused so quickly. It was more than foolish, for he had noted the attractiveness of the girl before he had married her. And now, as he had told her at dinner, there was no escaping the union. They would not be parted until death.

The realisation overwhelmed him and with it the futility of his plan. She had been wiser than he allowed when she'd informed him that much could change over the course of a lifetime. Why had he imagined that it would be possible to keep himself apart from her for decades if he was already failing after days?

Perhaps he simply needed a distraction. Vigorous physical activity during the day would exhaust him so that, by evening, he would sleep, rather than thinking of the woman laying just a room away.

He summoned some footmen and went down to the outbuilding where the yard games were kept and located a dusty set of bows and arrows and the straw target that went with them. Then he had the servants set up a creditable range on the back lawn.

He pulled an arrow from the quiver on the ground and fitted it in his bow, raising it and drawing back slowly. He sighted and released. The arrow cut through the air in a smooth arc, landing just shy of the centre of the target. A little practice would improve his aim. And what had he to do with his time but practice?

But the process itself, of slowly coiled energy and sudden release, was not so much calming as evocative of the very act he had been trying to forget.

'What are you doing?'

His hand stopped as he reached for the next arrow, surprised that she had approached without his hearing her. But at the sight of her, he felt an unwelcome lifting of his spirit and an uncontrollable urge to smile.

'A little target practice,' he said, looking back to his arrow. 'Nothing more.' He left fly with another bolt that came even closer to the centre of the target.

'Do you often practice archery in the garden?' she asked.

He hesitated. She was still trying to dig out the details of his life. It made him wonder why he was so unwilling to share, even when confronted by a question as simple as this one. Did he often practice archery? The correct answer to that was no. But if he told a small lie, it would seem less unusual. 'As often as I can,' he said.

'How very interesting.' He watched as she ran a tentative hand over the fletching on one of the arrows. 'And is it difficult to learn such a sport?'

'It can be. But one improves the more one practices,' he said.

'That explains why you are so accurate,' she said with a nod.

'Actually, the last two shots were more luck than anything else,' he said, not wanting her to expect a marksmanship he could not reproduce.

'So, you admit to being lucky, on occasion,' she said, the corners of her lips twitching as she tried not to smile.

It had been a bad choice of words, for it fed into her curiosity. 'If you are asking if I assume a family curse can affect the course of an arrow, no, I do not. But generally speaking, you will find that I have no particular skill as a marksman and do not hunt or fish because of the previous lack of success.'

'A moving target is harder to hit than a standing one,' she said, staring down the field at the straw disc.

'How would you know if you have never tried?' he said, feeling an unexpected swelling of confidence at knowing a thing that he might teach her.

'Would you allow me to shoot?' she asked, surprised.

'If you are inclined to do so, I see no reason you cannot,' he said. 'I do not know that this bow will suit you, but it will have to do for the moment.' He set his own bow aside and handed her the other of the two weapons that the footman had brought for him to try. The draw was lighter than the one he was using, but it was still a man's bow, meant for a man's strength.

To his surprise, she pulled the string back easily and held it with a steady hand. It seemed that she had the strength of an Amazon to match her height. 'Hold it thus,' he said, adjusting the position of her arms. 'And be sure to keep your elbow like so, to prevent a slap from the bowstring.' He stood behind her now, his hands on hers, and felt a slight shock as his arm brushed the side of her left breast.

If she noticed, he could not tell. Instead, she seemed focused on the advice he was giving her. 'I see.' She adjusted her posture as he had directed, then eased the string back again and grinned at him. 'But it is no good without an arrow.'

'Very true,' he agreed and showed her how to nock the arrow on the string. Then he stepped back, his hands on her shoulders, sighting down the length of the shaft to help her aim. 'A little to the left, I think. And remember to aim higher than you think you need to, as the bolt will fall in flight.'

In front of him, he could feel her body tensing and the breath she released as she let the arrow fly. It struck the target a few inches wide of his own. He had not expected she would hit the thing at all, but she held the bow with the grace of Artemis and did not hesitate as she shot. Apparently, her athletic build gave her a natural affinity for sports that did not carry over to the drawing-room mistakes she was always apologising for.

'Well, done,' he said, and squeezed his hand on her shoulder in a gesture of friendship that would have been fraternal, had she been a man. But since she was not, it was strangely intimate, and very pleasant.

'That was wonderful,' she said, dropping the bow and turning in his arms to face him.

Suddenly, the posture he had taken, meaning to be nothing more than a teacher guiding a pupil, had turned into an embrace. Her face, so close to his, was lit with a joyful smile, her lips parted and welcoming.

He was going to kiss her again. He knew he should not. To do so was to tempt fate and to raise false hopes. She did not deserve to be teased. Nor did he want to start something he knew he did not dare finish.

But suddenly, the urge was stronger than common sense and years of bitter experience at how much it might hurt to grow close to someone only to lose them. He wanted her. She was his. There was nothing as important as that. He leaned in and touched his lips to hers.

There was no hesitation in her response. As she had with archery and any other challenge he set for her, she threw herself into it with enthusiasm and a surprising amount of natural ability. Her mouth opened to his and her breasts pressed against his chest, as if begging for the touch of his hands.

He balled his fists, trying to resist the urge to caress her. Then, he surrendered to just a small part of what he wished to do and cupped his hand at the back of her neck, pressing his mouth to hers, sealing the kiss and thrusting his tongue into her mouth, drinking in the sweetness of her.

Her hands crept to his waist slowly, as if afraid that she would startle him away. When he did not release her, she grew bolder, pressing her body against his and moving against him as if she was trying to arouse him.

And it was working. Just as he had feared, now that he had begun, he did not want to stop. Yet, he must.

He stepped back and dropped his hands to his sides.

She looked even better for having been kissed. The flush of exercise had deepened to a full blush and her eyes sparkled with pleasure.

'Well,' she said, and her plumped, pink lips curved into a smile. 'That was even better than archery.'

'It will not happen again,' he said firmly. 'I was momentarily overcome.'

'I see,' she said and her smile faltered. He wondered if he had hurt her. But there was something other than disappointment in her expression. She suspected he was lying and that there was something more brewing between them. Then, she said the words he hated to hear from her. 'I am sorry.'

He should tell her that it was not her fault. What was happening had more to do with his overestimation of his strength than any seduction on her part. But instead of freeing her from any guilt in the incident, he turned and walked away from her.

It will not happen again.

It was not what Emma had hoped to hear, though she could not say that she was surprised by it. It was what he had promised from the first.

But he had kissed her. And without noticing it, earlier he had touched her breast. It had been all she could do not to jump in shock when it had happened. But if she had, he might have apologised and released her even sooner.

What she had not expected to hear was the other announcement.

I was overcome.

Never in her life had she thought she might be the sort of girl who drove men to take rash action, against their better judgement. It was the nicest compliment he could have paid her and she had come very near to thanking him for it. Then, she had realised that if reminded, he would likely deny it, and had apologised, again. It was a lie, of course. If she'd done something to cause what had just happened, she wasn't the least bit sorry.

Now that the information was out and he had admitted an attraction to her, she might find a way to use it. If she had been husband hunting, her mother might have advised her on what to do to fan a tentative flame. But very few women could counsel on what to do with a husband, once caught, who wished to remain tepid when you harboured warm feelings for him.

For a moment, she was sure they had been close to something more than just a kiss. But then he had regained control. And before she could think of a way to hold him, Robert had walked away, stiff and formal, as if nothing had happened at all. He had left her with those ordinary bows and arrows, when she needed not target practice but the skill of Cupid to get his attention.

She had not even bothered with another shot, since there was no point in practising if he was not there to hold her in his arms to correct her aim. Instead, she had instructed the footmen to put the equipment away and walked back to the house to see if she could find him again.

But when she had arrived there, she had discovered her family's carriage waiting on the front sweep. Her throat tightened. Her mother had promised her an entire month of privacy before the first visit. But it had not even been a week. Was something the matter at home? Perhaps there was something urgent, something wrong with one of her parents that she needed to hear about.

But the butler instructed her that her mother was waiting for her in the receiving room and did not seem agitated in any way.

When Emma came into the room, the woman was as cheerful as ever. She stood and came to gather her close for a hug, then held her away, declaring, 'Marriage suits you, my dear. Your colour is good. If possible, you look even taller than before.' This was said with a hint of disapproval, as though her mother had hoped that leaving home would somehow reverse the effects of nature.

'I am just fine,' Emma assured her, shaking free of her grasp. 'But what brings you to visit me? When last we talked, we agreed that I would not be ready for company for a few weeks yet.'

'I could not stay away,' her mother said, smiling eagerly. 'There was hardly any information in the one letter you sent me.'

'Because nothing had happened, other than the fire,' she said. Then added, 'Nothing has happened as yet to warrant more correspondence.'

'Then you must let me help you with your household duties,' her mother insisted. 'There are no doubt staff to interview, menus to approve and a gala of some kind to plan.'

'The menus are chosen. The staff is exemplary and does not need adjustment. The house practically runs itself. And as for galas...' She was not sure what to think of this, but she knew what her reclusive husband would likely say about such a thing. 'I will let you know the time and the place of our first entertainment, if we decide to have one.'

'A tour of the house, then. There was no time on your wedding day. And since the first moment I saw it, I have been dying to see inside,' her mother admitted.

'But marrying me off to the owner was a rather drastic way to achieve that end,' she said, shaking her head in amazement.

From the hall, she heard a throat cleared in warning and, a moment later, her husband appeared.

'Sir Robert,' her mother cooed, oblivious to the embarrassing discussion that had been interrupted. 'How good to see you again.'

'And after so long,' he said in a dry tone that was also lost on her.

'I was just going to give Mother a tour of the house,' Emma said, another apology on the tip of her tongue.

Robert nodded. 'If you need me, I will be in my study.' This was said in a way that indicated what room the tour should avoid. Then he continued on down the hall as if nothing had happened.

I'm sorry.

She didn't say it out loud, but she suspected he heard it anyway. Then she led her mother out of the room, in the opposite direction from the one her husband had taken.

Chapter Ten

Though she had not seen him at breakfast or luncheon, her husband appeared that night at dinner, but she could tell by the look on his face that he was unhappy with the way the day had gone. Was he annoyed that he had lost control and kissed her? Or was it the visit from her mother that bothered him?

They ate the entire meal in an awkward silence and as it dragged on, the clink and scratch of utensils on plates seemed deafeningly loud. Emma's nerves stretched thin as she searched for a topic of conversation that might break the silence. Then she remembered yesterday's argument and thought the better of it, waiting for her husband to speak first, though he showed no signs of doing so.

It was not until dinner was over that he seemed ready to unburden himself. He was staring into his wine glass, frowning. Then looked up at her over the rim and there was a change in the air between them, as if he was choosing his next words with care.

He was about to scold her for something. She hoped it was not the archery, for she did not think that had been her fault. But whatever it was, she wished she had not done it. She was used to her mother's quick rebukes, not this endless, disappointed silence. 'I'm...'

He held up his hand to stop the apology before she could make it. 'I understand that your mother is interested in this house and eager to see you entertain in it.'

If there had been any doubt before, he certainly understood it after what he must have heard today.

'Despite what she may think, the fact that I took your dowry does not entitle her to set the social itinerary for my home. My opinion on such things has not changed since the before our marriage. We do not entertain in Gascoyne Manor. There will be no balls, no house parties, no gatherings.'

She started in surprise. She was used to having her mistakes corrected, but she had not expected to be lectured over a thing she had not actually done. 'I have not requested any such thing,' she reminded him.

'Not yet,' he countered. 'It is one thing to accept a few invitations and visit the neighbours. But when the time comes that you succumb to your mother's requests and begin to petition me for the right to throw some gathering or other, the answer will be no.'

'Because of the curse,' she replied, with a sigh.

'The reason for it does not matter,' he said. Outside, thunder rumbled as a dramatic punctuation to his words. 'I am the master of this house and I do not wish you to entertain. That should be reason enough.'

'But without further explanation, your rules appear to be arbitrary,' she said. 'It is impossible for me to understand you if you will not explain yourself.'

Perhaps it was the flickering of a candle, but his face changed, as if he was considering her demand. Then, it was gone. 'You do not need to understand me to obey.' There was a flash of lightning and another ominous rumble.

'I have not as yet disobeyed you,' she said, frustrated. 'It is not as if I am eager to entertain. I doubt I will be any more successful as a hostess than I am as a guest. But at least I will admit to the things I am afraid of. Now tell me what it is that is truly bothering you.'

He opened his mouth to speak. But before he could, there was a great flash and a simultaneous boom and crash that sent a shudder through the house. In the following moment of profound silence, Robert rose from the table and went to the window.

'You said that you would believe I was cursed if smote by Zeus,' he said with a smile and motioned to her to come to his side. Once there, she could see the wreckage of a lightning-struck oak tree, lying on the ground outside.

'I was not personally struck,' she reminded him, regretting her earlier choice of words.

'But your prediction was startlingly accurate,' he said.

'It was not meant as a prediction. It was an analogy.'

'But spot on, all the same.' But he seemed

more amused than frightened by this latest problem.

'As she stared out at the tree, rain began to pelt the windows, streaking the glass to hide the smouldering ruins of the oak in the garden. 'It was certainly dramatic. But I do not see it as evidence of a curse in action. Was there significance to the tree? Was it planted by someone important? Did it hold meaning to you or to your family?'

'No,' he admitted. 'It was just a tree.'

'And we were startled, but not hurt,' she reminded him. 'It is much less severe than the tales of death and ruin that you told me before.'

'Death and destruction are nothing to hope for,' he reminded her.

'And ordinary problems are not signs of divine retribution,' she said. 'You will not be the only man to lose a tree in this storm. But you are the only one trying to attach a meaning to it.'

Or was he? She could not help feeling that, rather than brooding on doom, in this case he was just toying with her to distract her from something else.

'You are probably right,' he agreed. 'Sometimes, a lightning strike is just a coincidence. But now the storm is growing worse and there is nothing more to see from these windows. Let us retire to the sitting room and entertain ourselves in comfort.' Then he smiled at her.

The brilliance of it took her breath away and chased all thoughts from her head. Or almost all of them. There was something he had been about to tell her, she was sure. Then lightning had struck and the moment was gone.

But whatever it was might lead to another argument. Then he would not be looking at her as he was now, as if it would make him the happiest man in England to escort her to the sitting room. So she blushed and nodded, and let him escort her out of the room.

Once they had settled for the night, she offered him the deck of cards she had been playing with on the previous evening. 'Do you fancy a game of piquet?'

His smile faded as he arranged a table between their two chairs. 'Very well. But you will find I am as unlucky at cards as I claim to be at other things.'

'Living alone you are no doubt out of practice,' she replied.

'My grandfather forbade it,' he said. 'He only took over the raising of us because of Father's gaming and said it was the ruination of the family.'

It was then that she remembered his mention of his father's suicide. 'We do not have to, if it offends.'

He shrugged. 'It is not so serious as that. I am an indifferent player. But it might amuse you to win for an hour or so.' He spoke as if his losing was a foregone conclusion.

As play commenced, it appeared he was right. He did not win, no matter how promising the hand he was dealt or how miserable hers might be. At first, she suspected he was letting her best him to bolster her confidence. But then she watched him closer and had to agree with his initial assessment. He was simply not very good at the game.

While she had been raised by her mother to view cards like business, he had been taught what rules he knew as if they were a necessary evil. Hence, she discarded with care and kept a close eye on his doings to guess the contents of his hand. But his mind was elsewhere. He sometimes lost track of his own cards and paid no mind to hers at all.

If this was the family method of play, she could see why his father had ended a bankrupt suicide and why his grandfather did not encourage gaming. She could also see why a proud man would rather blame supernatural bad luck than admit that he was unable to bend a deck of cards to his will.

But if he truly believed he was cursed, there had to be more to the story than downed trees and bad luck. 'When did the curse begin?' she asked, dealing out another hand.

'What do you mean?' he asked, taking his cards and frowning.

'With these things, I am given to understand that there is something instigating a curse,' she replied, arranging her hand and looking up at him. 'Did a member of your family offend a fortune teller, or some other person of power?'

'What a ridiculous notion,' he snapped as they began to play.

'No more so than the curse itself,' she replied. 'But if you believe it exists, then surely you have given thought to when and why it began.'

He paused, as if trying to decide what he wished to tell her. Then, he said, 'I have felt its effects since I was a child, but my grandfather explained what was happening to me when he took me in. I assume, if there were more to the story, he'd have told me then.'

'And that was when you came to be cared by him,' she said. 'How old were you at the time?'

'Twelve,' he said, frowning down at the cards as she took another hand. 'And Jack was seven.'

So, his first introduction to the family legend had been when he was young and still reeling from his father's suicide. No wonder he clung to it so tightly. 'Do you mind if I look into the matter?'

'In what way?' he said, gathering the deck and squaring the corners so he could shuffle it.

'You have the family bible to show me the deaths. But surely there are other journals or diaries from the family that would have some explanation.'

'Perhaps,' he said. 'Such things are kept in the study.'

'Do you mind if I read them?'

'Not at all,' he said. 'Though I doubt you will find any way to stop it, there is no harm in you looking.' He stared down at the cards. 'Another hand? Or have we played enough to prove my point?' She had beaten him five times in a row and it was clear from the look on his face that this was the last way he wanted to pass the evening.

'I should have chosen the stakes before starting the game,' she said. 'I would be quite wealthy by now in the thing I most desire.'

'And what might that be?' he asked, smiling and laying down his cards.

'Kisses,' she said, changing the subject to distract him. 'And they needn't even be like the one you gave me in the garden. Last night's kiss was quite nice as well.'

She was not sure if it was an illusion of the firelight, but it appeared that her husband was blushing. He took a hurried sip of his port before responding. 'Then you must give me a chance to win them back. Chess, I think. I am much better at that. Do you play?'

'Well enough not to embarrass myself,' she said, as he poured himself another glass of wine.

'Then I will let you make the first move.'

As the game progressed, he proved that cards were his only weakness in strategy. His chess game was masterful and he gave no quarter on the first game, testing her strengths and weaknesses before declaring checkmate. The second game, he ceded her two pieces to make the play more equal, then beat her again.

By the time they were ready to retire he had beaten her three times. As they walked towards their rooms, he said, 'I trust I have won back anything I lost at cards.'

'If you wish,' she said, disappointed that he was so eager to avoid a goodnight kiss. 'But I would think that a game like chess would be worth more than a hand of cards. You have earned any forfeit you would like to take.'

They were standing in front of her door now and he laughed, low in his throat. 'A forfeit. That is a very dangerous thing to offer me.' Then, he leaned towards her in a way that was not quite menacing, but frightened her in a way that was hard to explain.

'What do you want?' she whispered, trying not to hope.

'The only thing worth wanting is the thing one cannot have,' he said with a sigh. 'And if I take it now, I cannot tell myself that my motives come from a momentary failing of will.'

'Then I have made a mistake by giving you time to think,' she said. Before he could get away, she lunged forward, threw her arms around his neck and kissed him on the mouth.

For a long moment, he made no movement in response and she became convinced that she had done it wrong. She knew little about flirtation and even less about seduction. Trying to be the instigator had simply proved how hopeless she was.

But when she was ready to give up and apologise, his arms came around her, adjusting her lips on his so that he might kiss her back. Then he cradled her against his body as his mouth opened over hers.

He tasted of wine and something else hot and heady that coursed through her body. It made her breasts ache to be touched and fire burn deep in her belly. She pressed herself tightly against him, swaying slightly to try to ease the longing, but instead it grew stronger, making her moan with frustration.

'Now you know how I feel when you are near,' he said, running his knuckles along the edge of her bodice, his fingers trailing on the exposed skin above it.

'Then why do you still resist?' she whispered.

'Because there are things more important than fulfilling my own desires,' he said with a sigh, stepping away from her. 'And now I am going to my room, for I have business to attend to. I suggest you do the same.'

Then he was gone before she could ask him what he could possibly need to do at such a late hour when normal people were in bed.

Chapter Eleven

Just as Emma had promised, the Weatherby musicale was likely to be a thoroughly boring evening, yet Robert felt the hairs rising on the back of his neck at the thought of attending it. Had it really been so long since he was about in society that such a simple outing raised the spectre of panic?

Perhaps it worried him that he would not be going alone. The idea that he was to be seen as half of a couple again was still very new. During his first marriage, going about in society had been so easy that he'd not even had to think about it. His late wife had been the daughter of a knight and would have been totally at home with the sort of people they would be meeting tonight. Her calm assurance had settled his nerves.

When he had remarried, he had not considered the different needs of his new wife and the way they might affect him. Even if she was not to be a hostess, she would have to struggle to carve a place for herself in a society that might be critical of her birth. And though there was little he could do to help her, he would have to watch her succeed or fail.

On the day of the musicale, she seemed to grow more and more nervous with each passing hour, bumping into walls as she walked past him and rattling her china at breakfast. As he walked past her bedroom, he caught her and her maid, heads together in debate, with half a wardrobe of gowns arrayed on the bed. Though all the garments looked equally attractive to him, apparently, women could see things that men could not.

In the end, a choice was made for Emma appeared on the stairs in a fetching green dress, her red hair piled high on her head and adorned with tiny emerald pins. He offered his hand to her and, after a moment's hesitation, she took it and let him lead her to the carriage. Then they set off to visit the Weatherbys.

* * *

If he'd had any trepidation before the event, it evaporated once they arrived. The gathering was small, no more than twenty people joined to hear the soloists who, Lady Weatherby assured them, had come all the way from London to provide the entertainment. The refreshments were little more than champagne and cake, which the guests took to their seats which were arranged in rigid rows at the front of the pianoforte. The combination was a recipe not for drama, but an evening of mind-numbing boredom.

At least, it was for him. But as he watched, he learned the reason for his wife's care in choosing everything about her debut gown. As the hostess introduced her, the other ladies scanned Emma from head to foot as if searching for obvious flaws. Though none was apparent, no one seemed eager to be the first to engage her in conversation. Each behaved in a pleasant but distant manner, as if waiting for another to declare the newcomer socially acceptable.

It annoyed him. Of the other guests, his own rank was nearest that of Lord Weath-

erby. That gave these lesser women no right
to question the pedigree of his wife. But apparently, their doubt was all it took to create
doubts in Emma. As he watched, her smile
changed from one of eager welcome to the
hesitant expression of one left waiting at the
door for others to take their place ahead of
her.

He was surprised by the surge of protective
anger he felt when he looked at her, but could
think of no way that he might help. Though
she had chosen an event that would not be
too taxing for either of them, there was also
no opportunity to call attention to her rank
as Lady Gascoyne. She would be forced to
rely on self-confidence to rule the day and
she had scant little of it.

Before the first soloist, he went to her and
took her hand to guide her to a seat and they
listened in silence together. At the end of
the song, he applauded politely. Beside him,
Emma was much more enthusiastic, letting
out a sigh of satisfaction.

'You are enjoying the performance?' he
asked, not precisely surprised, but gratified.

'Very much so,' she said. 'It has been some

time since I was in London and I miss the entertainments that are found there.'

Was this meant to be a criticism of his desire to remain at home, or simply a statement of fact? When he looked into her eyes, he could see no hidden motive in their expression. But there was something about the innocent eagerness there that made him regret he could not give her what she wanted.

At intermission, they rose to mingle with the other guests. And as they had been before, the other women were polite but aloof to Emma, as if they were still not sure what to do with her. She was equally polite, but standoffish with them. It did not help that, as she stood in their midst, she towered over them like the only swan in a flock of ducks.

From across the room he sipped his wine and willed her to distinguish herself in some way. When she put her mind to it, she was delightful company and it pained him to see her struggle.

She was speaking to the hostess now, relaying her rapture at the soprano duet and daring to allow a trace of her personality to show.

Her hands fluttered in the air as she remembered the music. Did she gesture too broadly? Or was it the fault of the woman next to her, who took a quick step away as if she feared she could be struck? The exact cause of what happened next was hard to discern.

There was a flurry of movement among the ladies, blocking a passing footman who was carrying refreshments towards the dessert table. To avoid the crowd, he turned wide, stumbling over his own feet. The pitcher of lemonade he held slipped from his hand, travelling in a graceful arc, its contents spewing outwards to splash down the front of Emma's gown, soaking her.

There was a moment of horrified silence followed by an embarrassed giggle from one of the younger ladies and hurried shushing from the older ones.

Emma stood dripping in the middle of the group, the rest of which were miraculously spared a drenching. Her face was red with embarrassment as rivulets of sweet, sticky lemonade ran down into her bodice, then down her skirts to puddle at her feet. 'Oh, dear,' she said at last. 'I am so sorry.'

Robert hurried to cross the room to help her, drawing his handkerchief from his pocket, though the linen was far too small to have any real effect on the problem. But before he could reach her, she had been hustled to the ladies' retiring room, leaving a trail of drips in her wake.

A short time later, Lady Weatherby returned to the music room and informed Robert that, though attempts had been made, the damage to her gown was irreparable and Lady Gascoyne wished him to get the carriage and take her home.

Robert collected her at the door of the retiring room and they walked to the carriage in silence. Despite the furious mopping and wiping, the smell of lemons still hung in the air around her. Once inside there was another profound pause as he tried to think of anything he might say that would make her feel better.

Then, she blurted, 'I am so sorry.'

'You are sorry?' He had waited too long and now she was blaming herself for the accident.

'I have ruined the evening,' she said, 'and my gown as well.'

Actually, the evening had gone much better than he'd feared it could. There had been no sign of the curse, even during the accident. But it might be better to let her think that any fault was his. 'There is no reason for you to take the blame for anything more than insisting that we attend. I warned you that any outing with me would be risky,' he said.

'Because of your bad luck?' she said as if the idea had never occurred to her. 'If that is the best your curse can do, then I doubt its significance.'

Her spirit was returning, as was her tendency to argue with him. He smiled. 'If I agree to that, then you must admit that the evening was not ruined by something that could have happened to any of the other guests. It was not your fault that you happened to be standing near the table when the footman spilled the drinks.'

'I startled him,' she said, her hands clenched in the wet skirt at her lap.

'If the servants at the Weatherby home are so easily frightened, they should not be serving at parties.' He reached across the carriage and laid a hand on hers, squeezing them gently.

The gesture seemed to comfort her and she relaxed her grip, turning her hands palm up and stroking his wrists with her fingers.

It had been a long time since he'd held a woman's hand. He'd forgotten how nice the simple gesture could feel. He closed his eyes for a moment, focusing on the warmth of her skin and the gentle, tentative touch of her fingertips. But when he opened them again, he could still see the worry on her face.

'It was not going well, even before the accident,' she whispered. 'They treated me as a curiosity.'

'They do so at their own peril,' he reminded her. 'I am one of the highest-ranking men in the county.'

She laughed bitterly. 'Because I will withhold invitations from them? The threat is meaningless if you do not wish me to open the house to guests.'

He frowned. It had never occurred to him that accepting invitations might lead to issuing them in return. But now was not the time to start another argument with her over a thing that had not yet occurred. 'The opinions of other ladies do not matter. I suggest you ignore them.'

'It would be easy enough to do so if I never had reason to see them again,' she said with a sigh. 'But if I accept any more invitations, I am likely to meet the same group of women at each of them.'

His first instinct was to announce the problem solved and tell her that they would not be going out again. But that would only confirm in her mind that this first outing had been a failure on her part. And, if the problem that occurred had been the fault of his bad luck, it was not so very serious that it justified a ban on all future outings.

'You must teach yourself not to care about what they think,' he said firmly, trying to encourage her. 'There was nothing wrong with your behaviour this evening before the unfortunate accident.'

'I was trying very hard to please,' she agreed.

He paused, considering. 'Then perhaps you should not try quite so hard. You must remember that the only person you need to please is your husband.'

'And do I please you?' she asked, hopefully. 'I do not see how I can for I have done nothing but argue with you since the first moment of our marriage.'

Perhaps that was true. But thinking back about it, her contrary nature did not bother him. He could hardly blame her for arguing over things that must make no sense to her. He drew her hand to his lips and kissed it. 'You please me very much.'

But in the dim light of the carriage lamps, she still looked lonely and miserable, huddled in the dampened dress that clung even tighter than usual to her curves. She needed comfort and more assurance than words could give. So he pulled her across the carriage and into his lap.

The weight of her was pleasant, as was the warmth of her against him. She moulded to him as if she belonged there, like some piece of his own body that had been missing and was just now returned. Deep within, he felt the first stirrings of desire.

She tried to squirm away. 'Now I will ruin your coat, just as I have my gown.'

He held her tighter, laughing softly. 'Then it shall be ruined.'

'I thought you said there were other things more important than this.' After his rejection the previous evening, this must be as confusing to her as it was to him. But it was one thing to succumb to weakness on her bedroom doorstep, quite another to snuggle with a woman who needed comfort in the carriage where nothing could come of it.

He sighed and tightened his grip on her. 'I said there were things more important than my needs. For the moment, let us talk about yours,' he said and kissed her gently on the cheek, wondering how best to help her. What she needed was to forget the disaster of the evening and lose herself, if only for a little while. 'As I said before, if you do not blame yourself for the incident at the Weatherbys', I will not blame it on my luck. It was an accident, nothing more than that. The next time we go out, it will be easier.'

'Thank you,' she said, her face lighting with an amazed smile.

For a moment, he forgot everything as well, except for those luminous blue eyes staring into his and the sweet mouth beneath them. Then he put a finger on her chin and turned her face to his so their lips met in an opened-mouth kiss.

She started in surprise, then relaxed against him as he gave her the kisses she longed for. He released her hands and wrapped his arms about her, then leaned her back into the squabs of the seat and gave in to temptation, letting his hands rove over her body.

As he cupped her breasts her back arched and she pressed herself into his hands, eager for more. They swayed together with the rocking of the carriage and she released a shuddering sigh as his lips slid to her throat, then to her breasts. He laughed and murmured, 'You taste of lemonade', as his tongue darted into the hollow between them.

He would likely regret this later. But for the moment, nothing mattered but the woman in his arms. Their problems floated away on a rising wave of desire as he moved against her, driving himself mad with the nearness of a pleasure he dared not take. Then she gave a sudden gasp of surprise that trailed away in a series of broken sighs that left her slumped against the seat.

He pulled away from her, surprised as well, then struggled to regain control of himself before things progressed any further. When he raised his head to look, her eyes were wide, confused and clearly embarrassed.

Still shaking, she slid out from under him and sat up, leaning into the back corner of the carriage seat, tugging at the neckline of her gown and trying to compose herself.

'Are you feeling better?' he said, trying not to grin.

'Yes, thank you,' she replied, glancing behind her as if wondering what the drivers might have heard.

'I am glad to hear it,' he said.

The carriage was pulling up in front of the house and, as it slowed to a stop, he reached past her to open the door.

Before he could help her, she leapt to the ground, leaving him alone and uncomfortably aware of the way her still-wet gown clung to her body, and the dampness of his kisses that still clung to her lips and breasts.

She turned back to look at him, clearly wondering if the interlude had truly ended, or if it might continue once they had arrived at a bedroom.

His smile was gentle now and shook his head. 'Go in the house, Emma, and let your maid help you out of your gown. I will see you in the morning.'

'I am sorry,' she said softly, but she sounded more puzzled than remorseful.

'You have no reason to be,' he said. 'Until tomorrow.' And he lifted his hand to his mouth and blew her a final kiss.

Chapter Twelve

Emma slept uneasily, dreaming of clandestine touches and heated kisses, and what might have happened if they had been at home near a bed and not riding in a carriage.

He had claimed that what he had done was for her alone. Perhaps that was why he had been able to stop so easily. But she had lain awake for hours, her body humming with pleasure and eager for more of it. If this was a hint of what he was denying her in not coming to her bed, it made her all the more determined to change his mind.

She did not see him at breakfast and suspected that he was avoiding her so as not to give her a reason to hope. But she told herself that it did not matter if he left her for a meal or two. He could not dodge her for a lifetime.

And that was how much time he insisted they would have together.

The last thing she needed was another visit from her mother, especially since that woman had decided to bring a friend along with her. The vicar's wife, a nervous little woman whom Emma had met briefly on the day of her own wedding, sat close at her mother's side and stared at Emma in baleful silence as if she realised that her presence was an imposition.

Emma cast a nervous glance in the direction of her husband's study, wondering if his caution that she not entertain at the house extended to morning calls from the neighbours. Then she sighed and chose to ignore him, just as he was ignoring her. It was not as if she could turn people away at the door when they arrived without looking even stranger than she felt as mistress of this house.

And in a way, Mrs Wilson's presence was her fault. She had been the one to suggest her mother take Mr Wilson and his wife in, after the fire. It was only polite for her mother to bring her along when making calls.

Before she could even greet them, her

mother clasped her hand and said, 'I heard that you attended a function at Lord Weatherby's home last night.' She leaned in, eagerly. 'Tell me all about it.'

'How do you know?' Emma said, not sure whether to be amazed or embarrassed at her mother's proclivity for gossip.

'There is not much that passes in the area that one does not hear of if one takes the time to listen,' she responded. But Emma suspected it was not so much the listening as the asking that gathered the information.

Which meant that her mother would hear of the lemonade incident, whether she told her or not. She sighed and relayed the story.

'You should not gesture so, when you speak,' her mother replied with a frown. 'I suspect that was what caused the problem.'

Robert had promised her that what had happened was not her fault. And then...

Then things had happened that she must not think about with her mother in the room. She fought down a blush and clasped her hands in her lap then replied, 'I will be more careful next time.'

'And be sure to invite the Weatherbys to

dinner. A small gathering, I think. No more than ten. Only the best people, of course. I can help you with the guest list, if you need.'

'No,' she said quickly, which elicited a raised eyebrow from her mother. 'I need no help with the list,' she corrected, not wanting to have to explain her husband's aversion to entertaining. 'I can manage quite well on my own.'

'If you really think so,' her mother said with a doubtful smile. 'But your behaviour at the Weatherbys does not support that.'

When she'd got up that morning she'd felt capable of moving the world. But now that she was talking with her mother, she was unsure again. Perhaps she wasn't capable of organising a dinner party. She had never done it before and just the seating arrangements could be a daunting task, with so many ranks and titles to remember.

Then she remembered that she was not allowed to have dinner parties, so the point was moot. 'No,' she repeated. 'I will need no help.'

'Perhaps it would be easier to start with a gathering that is already set,' her mother said, ignoring her denial. 'And we have come here to give you just such an opportunity. We have a problem and only you can help us.'

'Really.' She could not manage a better response, for she was sure, whatever the issue was, Robert would not want her involved in it.

'After the fire, the churchyard is a ruined and rutted mess,' her mother said, eliciting a hesitant nod from Mrs Wilson.

'And the annual midsummer festival is less than a month away,' the other woman said, wringing her hands.

'Since they cannot hold it in the usual place...' her mother started explaining.

'You thought that you would appeal to use the grounds of Gascoyne Manor,' Emma concluded for her, trying to hide her wince.

'You do have the land to manage it,' her mother said in a tone that said the matter had already been decided. 'And we know that if money is an object, your father can take care of it.'

Not only did she mean to host a major event on Robert's property, she meant to pay for it, too. It removed an objection, just as it added others. She doubted that Robert would want to be reminded of his recently constrained finances by receiving more help from her parents. 'That will not be necessary,' she said, then added, 'But I would have to talk to Robert, before any decision is made.' And she already knew what he would say when she asked him.

'How can he possibly object?' her mother said with a broad smile meant to bolster the worried Mrs Wilson.

'It is not in his nature to socialise in such large gatherings,' Emma said, trying not to reveal too much of his motivations.

'It is not as if he has to attend,' her mother reminded her. 'We simply need the use of his land.'

'The house will not be involved,' Emma said, almost to herself.

'Of course not. The whole thing will be no trouble at all.' She made it all sound so simple. And when her mother was in a mood such as this, it was difficult to deny her. She could wear down any opposition in no time at all.

'When is the date of the festival?' Perhaps

they were already committed and she would never have to explain this to Robert.

'A week from Saturday,' Mrs Wilson replied with a smile. 'Thank you so much for your help, Lady Gascoyne. I was at a loss as to what we would do. And this celebration means so much to the villagers.'

'I told you it would be no problem,' her mother said, patting the other woman on the hand. 'How could she refuse us?'

Though she had not actually agreed to anything, apparently her assent was now assumed. At a loss as to how to turn back the conversation, Emma replied, 'You are most welcome.'

The Harris carriage was in front of the house again and Robert tried to convince himself that he was not walking the grounds in an attempt to avoid his wife's mother. He did not actually dislike the woman as much as he abhorred her influence on Emma. He had no intention of denying her visits with her own family, but he did not want to encourage the older woman's obsession with his home. Nor did it seem that contact with her did her daughter's confidence any good.

But his own efforts to encourage her independence were dangerous as well. He had meant to reassure her with a few kisses after the debacle at the musicale. But, as they usually did when he got too close to Emma, things had got out of hand.

By the astonished look in her eyes in the carriage, she had never climaxed before. Perhaps that was why she had needed so little to take her to completion. He had been almost as surprised by it as she had been, worried by the knowledge he had given her. Now that she'd had a hint of what might happen, she might not leave him alone.

It was yet another reason that he was hiding in the midst of his orchard, far away from the house and listening to the soft thump of falling fruit. Orchard was an effusive description for what was little more than a small grove of trees. But it had been enough to provide a year's worth of apples to the estate for as long as Robert could remember.

But not this year. The Gascoyne orchard was blighted to the last tree. That meant there would be no cider pressing, no apple tarts and no sauces unless they purchased the fruit from another farm.

He wondered what Emma would say, should he choose to tell her. She would probably demand to know if this was the curse he had been speaking of. Then, she would want to know if the neighbours had similar problems. If so, did they attribute them to his curse or to the vagaries of farming and the fact that tree diseases might be as contagious as human ones?

Instead of annoying him, the thought made him smile. When she was not blaming herself for anything that might go wrong, she had a way of making his problems seem ordinary and easy to manage.

Of course, she still had not seen the worst of them and he hoped she never would. He had not suffered an attack since before their marriage. Perhaps she was the reason for it. For a moment, he allowed himself to toy with the idea that he might be free of his curse and live as other men did.

Then he rejected it. The fact that she made life easier did not mean he should grow to rely on it. He had thought the same thing during his last marriage, which had been blissfully free of incidents, only to have his problems come rushing back when he most needed to be free of them. If the loss of Elizabeth had taught him nothing else, it was how transient peace might be and how devastating it was to lose it.

It was why he had decided to keep his distance from his new wife, yet he had been failing dismally. He had not seen Emma since the previous evening, yet despite his hopes it had done nothing to diminish his desire for her. Worse yet, he missed her companionship. While he did not want to seek her out, there was no point in denying that when he went back to the house he would do so if only to tell her of this latest development, so she could dismiss it as nothing more than a normal twist of fate.

But it seemed he would not have to go to her, for she was walking up the hill towards him, head dipped and a wide-brimmed bonnet sheltering her fair face from the sun. In the open air, with no one to criticise her, she walked freely, taking long, easy strides to match the length of her legs. To see her move like this, he was aware yet again of how much she held back when around others and how hard it must be to fit in.

She was close now and, as she looked up at him, he could see something was wrong. She bit her lip and her pace slowed as if she was afraid to approach. Before she could even get within earshot of him, he could see her mouth forming the word 'sorry'.

He folded his arms and waited in silence.

'I know you told me that I was not to be allowed to entertain in the house...' she said.

'But your mother suggested it and you could not deny her,' he said with disgust, his soft feelings fading.

'It is not precisely like that,' she replied with a nervous laugh. 'And it is not as if we are to be throwing a ball.'

'Just what did you agree to?' Robert could not decide if what he was feeling was simply anger at being disobeyed, or some deeper, confusing emotion at the knowledge that, in a few short weeks, he had lost control of his life and his home.

'Because of the fire ruining the grounds,

there is no place to hold the midsummer festival. The vicar's wife wanted our help. There is so much land here. What could I have done?' his wife said with an innocent expression.

'You could have said no,' he replied. 'Or you could have called for me and I would have done it for you.'

'I did not think you wanted to be in my presence,' she said. 'We have not spent ten minutes in each other's company all day.'

'But that did not mean I wanted you to...' What had he wanted her to do? Since he had been hiding in the orchard rather than offering his opinion, he could hardly complain that she had been influenced by suggestions from others.

But that did not solve the problem of the church festival. 'We cannot have scores of strangers wandering the property,' he said. 'It is far too dangerous.' The musicale had gone well enough, but there was not a chance he could survive such a large gathering without incident.

'As long as they stay out of the bullpen, I do not see what can possibly happen to them,'

Emma replied, warming to the subject. 'The grounds are level and well groomed. It will not harm the landscape if a few tents are pitched and games are played.'

'But...'

'What if the curse takes someone?' she said, with a touch of scorn in her voice. 'If you think that the vicarage burned because you came too near to it, then you should be obligated to make up for the loss of the festival.'

She was trapping him with his own words and his unwillingness to explain what really might happen should he find himself in a crowd of people. But unless he meant to keep his wife locked in the house like a princess in a tower, he must accept that the outside world would be seeping into his ordered life in ways he had not expected. He sighed and held out a hand of compromise. 'Suppose I agree to this event...'

'You would not be bothered by it at all,' she said hurriedly. 'It is not as if you...as if we have to attend. I am assured that they have everything they need, except the place to hold it.'

He laughed. 'You know that is never the case. Speak to the housekeeper about what will really be needed in the way of servants and preparation. You will find that it is certain to take more work than anyone expects.'

'But they will not mind it,' she told him hurriedly. 'I have already spoken to Mrs Hill and she assures me the staff is up to the challenge and ready to help. They are very proud of the grounds and are eager for the villagers to see them.'

'Well, I wouldn't want to deny them, if the staff wants to entertain,' he said. It appeared that the matter had been settled before he had even been consulted.

She let out a relieved sigh, completely missing his sarcasm. 'You will not be sorry.'

'I am sorry already,' he replied.

Then she threw herself into his arms and kissed him quickly on the mouth, in gratitude. She pulled away again, just as quickly, covering her mouth in surprise at what she had done and waiting to see his reaction.

He grinned. His lips tingled and any troubles he might have with the festival were days away and not worth worrying about.

So he reached out his arms in a feint at grabbing her.

She laughed and dodged out of the way.

'You had best run,' he said, glancing towards the house and feinting again.

She laughed, then turned and tore down the hill towards the house. And he let her go, just to watch her run.

Chapter Thirteen

The day of the festival arrived and, despite Robert's hope, there was no sign of inclement weather, or other trouble that might require it to be cancelled. He had avoided all contact with the planning and organisation of the thing, thinking that if he did not know about it, it was less likely to bother him when it arrived.

So far, it was working. He watched from an upper window as tents and awnings were raised about the property and felt nothing more than idle curiosity and mild anticipation. The sky was exactly the sort of cloudless blue that any village child could hope for. Many of them were already running across the lawn, dodging in and out between adults setting up displays of prize produce and stands selling sugared buns and hot sausage rolls.

Of course, in avoiding the festival, he was also avoiding his wife, feigning more anger than he felt over her agreeing to the host the village on the property. Really, it was his own loss of control that bothered him most. When they were alone, he sought out excuses to kiss her, pretending that it was innocent flirtation that could be handled by seeking his release in private.

But her response in the carriage was clearly more than that. The awed look on her face as she had climaxed had amazed him. And the thought had risen that he might see that face again and again, if he would just yield and take her.

So after the kiss in the orchard, he had let her beat him to the house. Then, he had given her a peck on the cheek as a reward and gone to visit the graves of his late wife and son to remind him what dangers lay in getting too close. He must remember that there were things at risk far more important than fulfilling a momentary desire. He must keep her safe in the only way he could.

From his vantage point today, he could see her, her fair skin protected by a large straw bonnet, as she worked her way from group to group, making sure that they had everything they needed. Occasionally, he could hear her laughter along with a snatch of conversation, carried up on the wind from below.

Instead of the hesitance she displayed in more formal situations, she appeared confident and at ease in her role as hostess of the festivities. And he could tell, by touched caps and briefly bowed heads, that the villagers had accepted her authority. It was all as it should be, if his household and marriage were normal ones.

Looking down at her, he felt a pang of guilt at having trapped her into something less than she deserved. If she had married another, she might be doing just as she was now, but she would not have had to oppose her husband at each step of the process.

She would also have a man willing to love her as she deserved to be loved.

At that moment, she turned, looking back towards the house and at him in the window. Then she gave a broad wave of welcome to him, as if he needed an invitation to come to his own garden. Though he was too far away to see it clearly, he could imagine the smile hidden by the shadow of her bonnet brim.

He stared back at her, his hand gripping the windowsill. If there was going to be a problem, he thought he'd have felt some sign of it by now. But his head was clear and his heartbeat and breathing were normal. Could it do any harm to join the festivities? If things changed, he could always excuse himself and return to the house.

Slowly, he left his room and walked down the stairs and then outside into the bustle taking place at the front of the house. Once he was in the thick of it, the activity was almost too boisterous for him to stand. It was proof that he had spent too much time alone that a gathering as simple as this seemed loud.

He paused to steady his nerve, forcing himself to take deep, even breaths, and concentrated on the smiling face of his wife and her need for a successful day. He was standing in his own yard, on a bright sunny day. There was nothing to worry about. He would be fine, just as he had been on his last outing with Emma.

Before he could think further on the matter, someone had pressed a mug of ale into his hand. Mr Wilson, the vicar, was standing at his side, beaming in admiration. 'I cannot tell you how much it means to the village that you have opened your home to us, Sir Robert.'

'Well…' He gave an awkward cough and took a drink. Technically, he had done nothing of the kind. The house was still closed, as he'd always intended it to be. And the outside of it would not be in use if it hadn't been for Emma's prodding. 'You have my wife to thank for that,' he said at last. And, no doubt, her mother.

'The lovely Lady Gascoyne,' the vicar said, his smile growing even brighter. 'It is so fortunate that the two of you found each other. She is truly a blessing.'

'Yes, she is,' he replied automatically, because one did not deny such a thing after only weeks of marriage. And then, to his surprise, he realised that he was telling the truth. He glanced across the lawn to where she was rolling hoops with a group of children, laughing as if she was one of them.

She looked up and saw him staring at her. Then she passed her toys to the nearest child and came running across the grass to his side. 'I did not think you meant to join us,' she said, reaching out to take his hand and pull him into the fun.

'I did not plan to,' he admitted, unable to keep from smiling as he looked into her eyes.

'Well, I am sure everyone will be glad that you are here,' she said. 'They have all been asking after you and hoping for an introduction so they might thank you for your generosity.'

Since she had been raised by cits it was probably hopeless to request that she be less free with her acquaintance. It had been clear from watching out the window that she got on well with everyone. And now it appeared that she expected such benevolence of him, as well. 'That is most kind of them,' he said, at last, giving up on the hope that he might escape.

'And there are those of us who already know

you that might wish a moment of your time,' said an all-too-familiar voice behind him.

He turned to face his younger brother, standing beside a woman whom Robert presumed was his wife. And as it always did, when called upon to converse with Jack, he felt his throat tighten and his back stiffen, preparing for an argument. 'John.' The one word came out of him with difficulty and was accompanied by a rigid nod of greeting.

'Robert,' Jack responded with an ironic smile. 'I know we were not invited to your home, but I trust that today we are as welcome as the rest of the hoi polloi.'

'Of course you are welcome,' he responded automatically. 'It is an open gathering.' Inwardly, he winced, for he had made it sound as though his brother would not have been invited otherwise. In truth, he had not even considered that Jack might attend.

'But we were talking of introductions,' Jack said, interrupting his thoughts. 'Since you have not as yet met her, may I present my wife, Lucy?' He made the omission sound like it had been Robert's fault and not his own. But the marriage had been six months ago and Jack had made no effort to arrange a meeting.

'Mrs Gascoyne,' he said, as formal and awkward as if he was meeting a stranger and not a member of his own family.

'Sir Robert,' the young woman replied, her smile hesitant, as if she already assumed he would disapprove of her.

There was another pause, as the pair of them stared expectantly at him and he remembered that he also had an introduction to make. 'And may I present my wife, Emma?'

Unlike the timid greeting of the other woman, Emma seemed oblivious of the tension in the air and reached out to clasp the hands of the other couple. 'Major Gascoyne, how good it is to finally meet you. And your wife as well.'

'I take it we have you to thank for this celebration,' Jack said, greeting her with a warm smile.

'When the vicar's wife approached me with the request, I could find no good reason to refuse,' she said, eyes modestly downcast and a flush of embarrassment on her cheeks.

'I should think Robert would have been reason enough,' Jack replied, surprised. 'Under normal circumstances, he would never agree to such a thing.'

'Emma can be very persuasive,' he said, sparing her the need to lie and defend him.

Jack grinned, probably assuming that the negotiations had taken place in the bedroom. 'Well done, Lady Gascoyne. If you can evoke a change in my brother, then you truly are a miracle worker. And now, if you will excuse us, we will leave you to your other guests.'

When they had moved on, Emma turned to him with a brilliant smile. 'How nice it was to finally meet your brother.'

'For you, perhaps,' he said, staring after Jack as he moved off through the crowd.

Emma's smile faltered when she saw his expression.

'Do not think to apologise for not understanding my family problems,' he said. 'The difficulties between myself and him do not concern you.'

'I am sorry for them, all the same,' she said softly, touching his hand in reassurance.

He forced a smile. 'But we must not let them spoil your day. Show me the festival and convince me that I made the right decision in allowing it.'

At the end of the day, when the tents were being taken down, Emma was surprised to find that her first timid foray into entertaining had been a major success. Though she had done very little to organise it other than to open the gates and allow the people on the grounds, everyone seemed to think that she was responsible and showered her with gratitude.

They offered similar thanks to her husband, who accepted them with a dazed air, as if he was still not quite sure how he had come to have the entire village camped out on his property.

He must have been even more surprised to meet his own brother there, for he behaved most strangely towards him, as if he was not quite sure how to talk to his own family. And it was clear, despite the fact that they had been married for some time, that he had not met his brother's wife until today.

Best of all, nothing had happened that her husband might take as evidence of his bad luck. She turned to him, tugging on his sleeve. 'Now, admit it, the day has not gone as you feared it would.'

'There have been no problems that I have noticed,' he conceded.

'So, you admit it might be possible to entertain without a visit from your family curse,' she said, trying to keep the triumph from her voice.

'Such things are not predictable,' he said, dismissing her argument. 'That is why it is better not to tempt fate.'

'Well, in this case, the benefits have outweighed the risk,' she said, willing him to feel some enthusiasm for the day. 'And you must admit that you had a good time as well. Did I not see you playing horseshoes with the vicar?'

'He challenged me. I could not resist.' For a moment, he let down his guard and grinned, as he had when they were alone together.

'You could not resist,' she said with a nod, smiling.

Suddenly, someone on the other side of

the yard cried out in pain. At the sound, the colour drained from Robert's face and he raced in the direction of the noise, ready to help.

She hurried after him. When they arrived at the scene of the problem, it was nothing more serious than a childhood fight. She reached out to soothe the offended boy, then turned back to her husband, eager to prove him wrong. 'See? There was nothing to worry about after all.'

But he did not notice. He was clutching the nearest tent pole in one hand. The other hand was on his heart, as he struggled for breath. Though sweat beaded his brow, his face was still deathly white.

She reached out to steady him and felt his shoulders shake under her hand.

'Do not worry,' he wheezed and tried to straighten up. But as he released his grip on the tent pole, he pitched forward to his knees, unable to stand under his own power.

'Someone, help!' she cried as two footmen rushed forward, easing her gently out of the way, linking their arms with his and lifting him to carry him, unresisting, back towards the house.

* * *

It was the first time his wife had visited his bedroom and he could not imagine a more anticlimactic reason for it. He did not want her to see him this way, propped up by pillows like a damned invalid and under the influence of laudanum-laced brandy. But at the moment, he lacked the strength to refuse her.

She was sitting at his bedside, a worried expression on her pretty face, her hands clasped tightly in her lap. At least she was not patting his hand as if he was a sick child. 'The doctor says it is your heart and that you have had these spells before,' she said in a faintly accusatory tone.

'The doctor is an old woman. He knows nothing about what ails me,' he snapped. And he never would. If he understood the full extent of Robert's problems, he would have recommended a madhouse instead of rest and laudanum.

'Why did you not tell me that you had this trouble?'

'I told you often enough that I did not want to entertain,' he snapped. It was unfair of him to bark at her, when he was angry at his own weakness. He had known she would see the effects of the curse eventually. But he had not expected to pitch cataleptic at her feet when it happened. He'd not had an attack this bad since Jack had returned from the war.

She was clearly hurt by his tone, but she pressed on. 'But you never said you were ill. Why did you not tell me that entertaining taxed you so? I would never have agreed to the festival had I known.'

'I am not sick, nor am I exhausted,' he replied. 'There was nothing the least bit stressful about a round of horseshoes and a walk around the yard.' The festival had not been the problem. Although talking with Jack had been mildly unsettling, it had been the scream that had finished him. He had thought it was a woman's scream. It had reminded him of the night Beth had died.

'I suppose you are going to blame it all on the curse, again,' she said bitterly.

If what happened to him was not a curse, he had no idea what to call it. 'As I told you, the Gascoynes die young,' he said.

'You are not going to die,' she said. 'I will not let you.'

Her stubborn insistence did more for him than the medicine had and he laughed out loud. 'You will not let me die? If you have the power to choose the time of my passing, then I will have gained far more from this marriage than I expected.'

'I will not let you die over something as silly as cursed luck,' she said. 'And I promise not to bother you with any more entertaining…'

'Because you are afraid that I will faint like a girl and disgrace us both,' he finished her sentence for her. Hadn't that been what he was afraid of? And his fears had proved true.

'That is not what I fear at all,' she said. 'And you did not embarrass yourself or me. You simply frightened me because I had no warning.'

'You have no reason to be afraid,' he said. He had been quite frightened enough for both of them. As usual, his pounding heart and the inability to breathe had been accompanied by an irrational and blinding terror and the certainty that death was near. 'I am all right now,' he added.

But that was not true, either. As always, he was afraid that the uncontrollable feeling would come upon him again, without warning. And the next time, there might be no way to stop it. Perhaps he would die right in front of her, clutching his heart in terror, unable to help himself or anyone else.

She gave him a dubious look.

He set the brandy glass aside and denied his fears. 'I will be all right once the effects of the laudanum have faded.'

'For now, you need to rest,' she said. And this time she did pat his hand, as if he was a babe that needed coddling. 'And I am sorry for all the trouble I have caused you. I promise to be better in the future.'

He snatched his hand away. 'How many times must I tell you not to take the blame for things that are not your fault?'

'But you did not want the festival,' she reminded him.

'And I was wrong. Everyone enjoyed it and the day was a success,' he reminded her. At least it had been up to the moment when they'd had to drag him limp into the house. But that hurt nothing but his pride. Despite the nagging feeling that he was doomed, he would probably survive just as he had after past attacks. 'My opinions on entertaining have not changed. That said, I do not regret your involvement in it. It was the right thing to do.'

A smile spread slowly across her face and her body seemed to relax, as she remembered. 'It did go well, didn't it?'

He nodded and felt his head wobble as the laudanum began to take full effect.

'But we can discuss that tomorrow,' she said, rising to go. 'Right now, you need your rest.'

'I do not need rest,' he muttered. He patted the bed at his side and raised his eyebrows in invitation.

'Certainly not,' she said, drawing away with a frown. 'I will not come to you now when you can blame the opium for what happens between us. Now go to sleep and we will talk tomorrow. I am sure you will not want me in the morning.'

'...tomorrow,' he repeated as she walked from the room. She was wrong, of course. He would want her just as much. He would simply be too sensible to act on the feeling.

Chapter Fourteen

The previous day had been a strange one. Emma could not help but feel joy at the success of the festival, but it still made her feel guilty that it had come at such a cost to her husband. Of course, he might have had no problem if he'd warned her that he was prone to such spells, which the doctor claimed had occurred on and off since he was a child.

He had insisted that it was not his heart. But what else could it be? After running to help the child, he had clutched at his chest, as if it was about to burst. Perhaps it was the stress of the horseshoe game that had pushed him near to apoplexy.

He might claim it was a curse that kept him isolated from his neighbours, but now she knew better. She must take better care of him, and make sure he did not overtax himself for no good reason. She would begin immediately and make sure that he stayed in his room today and got the rest needed to fully recover. The doctor had recommended plenty of sleep and a diet of broth and milk toast, devoid of foods that might inflame the senses.

But when she went to his room to find him, it was empty except for the remains of a hearty breakfast of forbidden foods. His valet informed her that the master had gone for an early morning ride and had most likely returned by now. He suggested she seek him out in his study. But when she checked that room, she found no sign of him.

His absence frightened her. What if he had strayed too far from the house and had another attack? On such a large property, how long would it take someone to find him? Suppose they were too late to help?

Then she heard a strange noise coming from the ballroom down the corridor. It was a rhythmic *pok-patok*, repeating over and over, in a way that soothed her jangled nerves.

When she went to investigate, she found her husband in shirtsleeves, racquet in hand, playing tennis against the ballroom fresco.

As she watched, he tossed the ball into the air, serving it into the wall and leaping forward to slam it again as it returned to him. The continual sound she'd heard had been that of the ball meeting racquet, meeting wall and floor.

'Stop that immediately,' she said, her hand to her mouth in horror.

As the ball returned to him, he caught it easily in his left hand and turned to her, smiling. 'Are you afraid that I will collapse again?' He held his arms out wide. 'As you can see, I am not the least bit impaired.'

He did seem unbothered, even after strenuous exercise. But that did not change the fact that he had seemed near to death just a day ago. 'You might appear fine,' she allowed, 'but that does not mean you should tempt fate.'

He laughed. 'So, this is what it takes to get you to believe in fate.'

'I was not speaking of your curse,' she said.

He shrugged. 'Were we not? Because I cannot think of a better proof of it than what you witnessed yesterday.' He served the ball again and it slammed into the fresco hard enough to send a shower of plaster to the ballroom floor. 'I am as strong as an ox when no one is looking and weak as a kitten when they are.'

'And that is why you will not entertain,' she said.

He nodded. 'As long as I remain calm and alone, I am able to manage the problem. But in society, I cannot predict what might happen.'

'Perhaps, if you limit yourself to less strenuous gatherings...' she said.

He shook his head. 'You still do not understand. It is not the strength of my body that I need to worry about. The problem lies elsewhere.' He tapped his forehead.

'You think it is in your mind?' she said, shocked.

'The curse of the Gascoynes,' he replied with a nod. 'When I am confronted with a problem I cannot solve, or see others in danger and cannot help, I am overcome with terror so complete that I can hardly breathe.'

'Yet, yesterday, when you thought there was trouble, you ran towards it, not away,' she reminded him. 'And you were quick to rush to the aid of the vicarage fire. If you are afraid of the curse, when an opportunity presents itself to help, why do you take the risk?' she asked. 'One would think that any such activity would be more dangerous.'

'Why do I help people when they need it?' he said, surprised. 'Because, despite what you must think of me, I am no coward. If something dire happens to me as a result of my actions, then I am fully prepared to accept my fate. But what I cannot do is watch others suffer. If there is anything to be done, I must at least try to help.'

'You cannot solve all the problems around you,' she said with a shake of her head.

'But I have to try,' he said, more to himself then her. 'To be frozen in terror during a disaster and to distract the doctor from his duties with my own infirmities when there was someone else who needed him more? To be told after that there was nothing that could have been done? To be left helpless in the face of an emergency is by far the greatest curse that could be wished on a man.'

He was speaking of the death of his wife and child. As she watched, the hand that held the racquet began to tremble and his breathing changed, becoming laboured at the memory.

He shook his head, trying to clear it.

If he blamed himself for his wife's death, it explained his over-protectiveness when it came to this new marriage and his fear of becoming intimate.

'There will always be things that you cannot control,' she reminded him.

'And that is why I avoid people,' he replied, struggling to slow his breathing. 'If I cannot stop bad things from happening, it is easier not to see them.'

If just the idea of helplessness was enough to bring on another spell, she needed to find a distraction. She glanced at the ball in his hand. 'But none of this explains why you are playing tennis in the ballroom.'

He glanced down at the ball he was still holding and then at the ruined fresco that had been his target, as if he had not realised that there was anything odd about his behaviour. But his breathing had steadied by the time he answered. 'I thought, since the space was not being used for dancing, I would find another purpose for it.'

'Do you not have a tennis court on the property?' she asked.

'With no one to partner me, it hardly seemed worth the effort to open the room,' he said.

'At least now I know what happened to the painting on the wall. My mother will be appalled,' she said.

'You do not have to tell her,' he replied, with a smile.

'It does not matter whether we have a ball or who knows of what you are doing. As lady of the house, I must insist that you cease abusing this room.' For a moment, she had forgotten that she had no right to give him orders in his own home. But he did not seem to like it when she apologised without reason, so she held her tongue, waiting for his reaction.

To prove he was still the master, he served again and said, 'One last game will not make things much worse. There is a second racquet if you wish to join me.'

'I have not played tennis before,' she remarked, with a wistful look at the racquet in his hand.

He stepped forward and placed it in her

hand. 'Here. Let me show you.' Then he showed her the correct way to swing it, before demonstrating an easy serve, bouncing the ball off the wall to land at her feet. 'Now you try. Aim for the eye of that cherub on the left.'

She wouldn't dare. Yet it looked as though it might be fun. And it was clear that tennis took his mind off his troubles. If she did as he asked, she would be helping him as well as obeying. So, she picked up the ball and served it as he had shown her, coming within inches of her target on the first try.

He returned the serve, then stepped out of the way so she could hit it again.

She laughed as her racquet connected with the ball, then turned to him and smiled, surprised. 'I did it.'

'Of course you did.' He seemed just as pleased as she was. 'You are one of those people who take to sports easily. Has it always been so?'

'I do not know,' she said, frowning, unsure of the answer. 'I was told that they were unladylike and have never tried them.'

'And I suppose it was your mother who told you this,' he said with a knowing nod.

Of course it had been. 'But other women agree as well,' she said, thinking of the sedate ladies at the Weatherby musicale.

'As I told you before, you must learn to ignore the opinions of others who are telling you to be less than you are,' he said, picking up another racquet and serving the ball again.

Without thinking, she returned it and the game was on.

An hour later, she emerged from the ballroom invigorated. The fresco was in even worse condition than it had been, but she could not deny that she had most enjoyed destroying it. From what she could see, it had been ugly when it was newly painted and was not likely to get prettier with the passage of time.

Even better, her husband had played a game with her and it had been a game she had been good at. If she had made any missteps or mistakes, he had not berated her for them. Though she had been worried at first that he would have another spell, as the competition had grown heated, he'd shown no sign of flagging or even becoming winded and assured her that had he enough time for it, he could go on for hours without a problem.

Best of all, when he had seen how much she enjoyed it, he had promised that they would play future games on the tennis courts where they could do so properly. That meant there could be other mornings like this one, spent happily in each other's company without worry that she would do something to frighten him into ignoring her again.

As she walked down the hall towards the morning room, the butler interrupted her with news. 'Madam, Mrs Harris is waiting for you in the receiving room.'

Just as quickly as it had come, her lighthearted feeling evaporated into guilt. The last thing she wanted was another visit with her mother, critiquing her behaviour and quizzing her on Robert's health. But if she was already in the house, it was too late to avoid it. With hope, her husband had retired to his rooms and she would not have to explain the conversation that was likely to occur.

She went to greet her and her mother rose,

taking her hands and admiring her, with an approving nod. 'It is good to see you have survived your first attempt as a hostess.'

'Thank you, Mama,' she replied, though she was not sure if this was the correct response, since the comment was hardly a compliment. 'Was there really any doubt that I would?'

'Well, you know how you get,' her mother said in a dismissive tone. 'It was good to see that there were almost no problems.' She paused, then gave Emma a searching look. 'And is your husband feeling better, my dear?'

'Much better, thank you,' she said hurriedly.

'It was not caused by too much cider, was it? The drink served was not very strong, but it can take some by surprise.'

'Certainly not,' Emma said hurriedly. 'Yesterday was just a momentary turn. Nothing that need concern anyone.'

'Then that is what I will tell people who ask,' she said with another nod.

Emma's heart fell. It had not occurred to her how quickly gossip might spread and how extreme it might be. 'It is really no one's business,' she said, biting her nail.

'Stop that immediately, Emmaline,' her mother said automatically. 'And do not think you can prevent the neighbours from being concerned in your business. I dare say your husband has not managed to prevent gossip by being a man of mystery who never leaves the house. Going out is unlikely to make things any worse.' She gave her daughter another pointed look. 'You are going out, aren't you?'

'Of course,' Emma lied, giving her mother the answer she wanted to hear.

'Lovely,' she replied. 'And where are you going, next?'

The problem with lying seemed to be that it was impossible to do it just once. Now she had to come up with a second lie to cover the first. Emma struggled to remember what invitations she had received in the morning's post. 'The Pritchetts are having a dinner party,' she announced. This was perfectly true. She had received an invitation, though she had not actually responded to it. But it was not lying to say that the dinner existed.

'An excellent choice,' her mother said with

a smile. 'We are going as well and will see you there.'

'Lovely,' Emma said. Now, she would have to accept the invitation, unless she wanted to admit to the lie.

'It is good that you are getting out,' her mother said with an approving nod. 'As far as I have heard, you have not sent as much as a dinner invitation to anyone, much less a larger event. If you will not allow people in, then you must at least go out.'

'I was entertaining only yesterday,' Emma said, exasperated.

'Because I appealed to you to do it,' her mother responded.

'That was a special situation. Robert does not usually like to entertain,' she said. Now that she knew the reason she had been forbidden from doing so, she could see his point.

'We knew that the man was a recluse when we chose him for you,' her mother said with a sniff. 'But I did not expect his original feelings on the subject to remain the same after he was wed.' Then her mother gave her a coy smile. 'In time you will learn to twist him around your finger on such subjects.'

'I seriously doubt it,' Emma said, frowning.

At this, her mother laughed out loud. 'Then you do not know very much about marriage,' she said.

This was very true. 'I know that Robert does not want me to entertain,' she said. 'And I will show you the ballroom that was locked on your last visit. You will see that it is quite impossible to hold a gathering there, if that is what you mean for me to do.' Then she led her mother down the hall to show her the ruined fresco.

On seeing the room, her mother shook her head. 'I expected some problems with the house, but this is worse than I thought,' her mother said, staring at the plaster dust on the floor and the peeling cherubs. Then she glanced down at her feet and snatched up a tennis ball. 'Tell me you have not been playing children's games in a formal room.'

'Not I,' Emma said. Technically, it was not a game that was just for children, but the half-truth left her flushing with embarrassment.

'Your husband, then,' her mother said, shaking her head, then she pointed up at the painting. 'There is nothing to be done for that. It is ruined beyond repair. But why would he do such a thing?'

'He seemed to think it was easier than using the court,' Emma replied.

'Then it is a good thing he has married you,' her mother said with finality. 'You must put a stop to it at once.'

She already had. But was she really obligated to explain that to her mother while in her own home? But this momentary flash of defiance faded just as quickly as it had come when she looked at her mother's disapproving expression. She said, 'Yes, Mama', her embarrassed blush deepening.

Her mother awarded her with another approving nod. 'Men are like gardens, my dear. If left to their own devices, they get out of hand. They become unkempt, weed-ridden things. They do not like to admit it, but they need a hand, gentle, yet firm, to trim them into shape so they might achieve their full potential.'

'I do not think of Robert in those terms,' she said, trying to reassert some authority.

'You may think what you like, my dear, but it is not normal to play tennis in the ballroom, nor it is normal to shut the house to guests, or faint at public gatherings and then allow rumours to circulate about it.'

It was rude of her mother to say so. But hadn't she thought such things herself? 'And what am I to do about it?' she asked, at last, knowing her mother would tell her, no matter what she did.

'That is completely up to you,' her mother replied with a sigh that said there was really no choice at all. 'Of course, I know what I would do, in your circumstances. I would plaster over the damaged mural,' she said, staring up at the wall. 'Then I would inform him of the need to throw a ball and invite all the neighbours.' She clasped her hands together, obviously warming to the plan as she made it. 'He should invite his brother as well. Whether he knows it or not, the separation of the two is common talk in the village and an embarrassment to his family.'

Was there really threat of gossip in every direction she turned? It had been bad enough when her mother was worried she could not manage to step outside the house without making a cake of herself. Now, apparently, she was expected to manage the reputation of her husband, as well. 'But, Mama,' she said, 'Robert has made it quite clear that he does not want to hold a ball. And if he is truly separated from his brother, I cannot just fix a problem that has gone on for years that I had no part in making.'

'You do not know what you can set your mind to, until you try it,' her mother said firmly. 'At one time, I was quite in despair of you ever marrying and look how well I have done for you.'

'Thank you, Mama,' she said, numbly, trying not to wonder if a loveless marriage was truly the best that she deserved.

'But all this can wait until after you have attended the Pritchetts' party and proved that you can both get through an evening without creating some sort of unfortunate scene.'

'Of course, Mama,' she said, giving up. In comparison to a ball, a dinner party was really no problem at all. And as for a reconciliation of brothers? The best that could be done was hope that Mama would forget the whole scheme and not take matters into her own hands to try to fix things herself. Now that she was married, her loyalty should be to her husband and his side of whatever argument existed. She would stand by him, though he had not even bothered to tell her of an estrangement that the whole country seemed to know of.

Perhaps it would serve him right if she did decide to meddle.

Chapter Fifteen

Robert sat in his study, feeling better than he had in ages. He had needed a game of tennis, to prove to himself and Emma that he was fully recovered from yesterday's spell. But he had forgotten how much more satisfying it was to play against someone, rather than just volleying against a wall.

And for a beginner, Emma had been a worthy opponent. With practice, she would be even better and might be a challenge to best. Though pride had made him resist, he had to agree with her that the game would be better if played on a proper court. As she had suggested, he had given a footman instructions to reopen the tennis court.

It had been even more gratifying to see the way his wife had blossomed with her success. She had been obviously worried when she had found him exercising. But an hour later, she was laughing aloud, totally unconcerned as he slammed the ball against the wall to bounce at her feet.

That had been the biggest relief of all. He did not want her, of all people, to think him weak, even if he had just displayed that weakness to half the county. Perhaps it was true of all men and their wives, but it still surprised him that he had come so quickly to needing her good opinion.

But now, he glanced up to find Emma standing in the door of his study, hesitant to enter. Her earlier confidence was gone again and, by the look on her face, she was about to apologise for something.

He gestured her to enter and waited for her to speak.

'I have accepted another invitation. To the home of Mr and Mrs Pritchett. For dinner.' The words rushed out of her, then stopped, as if waiting in fear of a negative.

At the thought of another outing, he felt his hands growing cold. He dropped them beneath the desk and gave then a shake to return the blood to the fingers. 'And did you not think to ask me before making the decision?'

'It will give me a chance to show that the lemonade incident was merely an aberration,' she said, giving him a hopeful look.

'Surely that has been forgotten by now,' he said. 'You did very well yesterday.' Of course, he had not.

'Even so, we cannot spend all our time at home, alone. People will talk,' she said.

'They will talk even more so if I fall down in a fit while visiting their homes,' he said.

'Is it really the gossip you are afraid of?' she asked him, her gaze steady and direct.

'I am not frightened of the attack, if that is what you mean.' It was not quite a lie. He was terrified. The memory of yesterday was still fresh in his mind: the crushing feeling in his chest and the conviction that he was going to die at any moment. He could feel his lungs tightening at the thought of another evening with strangers so soon after the last incident.

'Of course not,' she said, obviously not believing him. 'But in case that was the problem, I have chosen a small dinner party, where nothing of interest is likely to occur. You should have no trouble braving the curse again. For my part, if it is no worse than another pitcher of spilled lemonade, I think I can manage.'

'I managed well enough at the Weatherbys,' he admitted. But he could not shake the feeling that a disaster was bound to happen.

There was a pause, as if his wife were choosing her next words with care. 'And I do not think it wise that the last view of you that people got was during your moment of difficulty. It would be wise to go about in public and show them that it was a passing thing that does not concern us.'

If he worried about what people thought about him, he would agree with her. He had given up caring for that, long ago. But her mother had trained her to obsess about the opinions of others. She did not precisely look eager for another outing, but it appeared that she had committed herself to it and was resigned to continue.

He sighed. 'Very well. We will go out to dinner. But if things end up worse rather than better, do not be surprised.'

* * *

Emma prepared for the dinner party as carefully as she had the musicale, obsessing over each detail of her toilette and practising acceptable topics of dinner conversation, to be sure that she would not be caught with nothing to say to her partners. She could not force the ladies of society to look on her as an equal. But this time, there would be no troubles that could be faulted to her and no gossip over her clumsiness or gaucherie. Her manners would be every bit as proper and her behaviour without flaw.

She wished that Robert's confidence would equal hers. He still tended to see the worst in any situation, but she must trust his denial that he had no fear of another spell. But if that depended on the evening remaining uneventful, she must try all the harder not to cause a problem that upset him.

The night of the dinner arrived and they presented themselves at the home of Mr James Pritchett, a gentleman of some means whose wife had a reputation for lavish entertaining. According to her mother, their money was old, their reputation good and their cook excellent.

Mrs Pritchett greeted her warmly, which was not a surprise. If her mother and father were already on the guest list, the hostess was not likely to be standoffish with the daughter of a cit. This time, it was her husband who was the object of curiosity, with the other guests watching him as if waiting for him to drop to the floor in a stupor at any moment.

In response, he showed no sign of noticing and no symptom of difficulty. He was as calm and collected as she wished she could be. When he sensed her watching him, he glanced across the room at her and gave her an encouraging smile and walked forward to take her hand and escort her to dinner.

Though the food was as good as her mother said it would be, she had wasted time in bothering to prepare topics for discussion. The company was dull and Emma found she did not have to work so hard at distinguishing herself if her end of the conversation was limited to listening politely to the gentlemen on either side of her and agreeing with everything they said.

On this evening, the companion on her right was Lord Fairfax, an older gentleman with a voracious appetite and a very high opinion of himself. Between his comments on the menu and his pontification on world affairs, she had but to nod in response to keep him happy.

Thus, it was surprising when, during the main course, his one-sided conversation stopped mid-word.

At first, she wondered if she had missed some verbal cue that a response was required and had left him waiting for her input. But when she turned to look at him, he seemed just as surprised by his silence as she was. His mouth was open, working as if searching for a word, but no sound issued from it. Then a flush began to creep up from his collar turning from deep red to purple as the air in his lungs began to foul.

'Lord Fairfax?' she said hesitantly, as the man put his hand to his throat, trying to loosen his cravat. 'Oh, dear.' The man was choking on his beefsteak.

She looked quickly from side to side, wondering who would be the most use in this situation. Her husband was across the table, thus out of reach. The lady on the other side of Fairfax had not noticed the sudden silence and the gentleman on her other side was pre-occupied with the partner on his left. But she was aware of the problem. Surely there was something she could do.

She stood up suddenly enough to rock her chair back and knock it to the floor with a bang. Around her, there were gasps of alarm and a shocked exclamation from the hostess. But she ignored them and turned to Fairfax, who was sagging forward in his chair. She hit him smartly between the shoulder blades, trying to dislodge the obstruction.

It was not helping. Perhaps she was not being forceful enough. She hit him again, harder. Still there was no change, other than that the man looked weaker.

In a last act of desperation, she thrust her hands under his arms and hauled him from his chair, dragging him forward to shake him.

The force must have been enough, for there was a huff of breath and the meat he was choking on flew across the table, knocking over her husband's wine glass.

The table fell silent, except for the sound of

Lord Fairfax, taking in deep gulps of air as his colour returned. Then, the room seemed to come to life, everyone speaking at once. From down the table, she heard a genteel shriek of horror from her mother.

Emma tried not to imagine the conversation they would have tomorrow and sagged back to sit on her chair. Or at least she attempted to do so. The seat she was aiming for was no longer there, for she had knocked it away earlier. She continued all the way to the floor, her bottom hitting the boards with a soft thump as chaos reigned above her.

His wife continued to astonish him. Another woman, when confronted with the sight of a man dying at her side, might have frozen in place. Worse yet, she could have fainted, or panicked, or got in the way of help, adding to the confusion rather than lessening it.

Instead, Emma had stepped into the thick of things and saved a man's life. Robert had not even had time to register the presence of a problem before Emma had fixed it.

Best of all, he had not added to the confusion of the evening with another spell. The incident had begun and ended so quickly that he'd had no time to react to it at all and was left watching from the side in surprise as Emma had handled the situation herself.

Now, they were in the carriage on the way home and, judging by her demeanour, she was not as impressed by her performance as he had been. 'I think, for purposes of our outings, it might be necessary to find a new definition for success,' he said, trying not to smile since the situation had been a serious one. But he could not help feeling an unexpected pride at the way she had behaved.

'It was a disaster,' she moaned, her hand shading her eyes from the lamp that lit their carriage.

'No one died,' Robert said. 'In fact, you were hailed as a hero for saving Fairfax. It was very quick thinking on your part to help him. Several of the other gentlemen told me how impressed they were.'

'The gentlemen might have spoken to you in approval, but the ladies did not say a word to me, other than to tell me that they never would have done such a thing,' she said, wincing.

'That is only because they think themselves unable to do something useful,' he said.

'And I did not know what else I could do,' she said.

'You could have asked for help,' he mused. 'But that would have taken time and Fairfax did not have it.'

'I made the right decision,' she said, obviously feeling no better about it. 'I just wish it would have fallen to someone else. I do not like being the centre of attention.'

'You will not always be so,' he reminded her, though the words were likely a lie. Because of her height alone she stood out from the crowd of other ladies. The fact that she seemed to attract drama only made it worse.

'I can hope,' she replied. 'But until that point, I am sor—' Before he could stop her, she corrected herself. 'No. I am not sorry. Not tonight.'

He smiled, for it was the first time he could remember her not being sorry about anything.

'I am embarrassed,' she corrected. 'But I will not take the blame for the fact that Lord

Fairfax ate too fast. He admitted so himself when speaking to me later and promises to be more careful in the future.'

'That is probably wise of him,' Robert agreed.

'I am sure the next time we go out, it will be without incident,' she said, looking more optimistic than before.

'The next time,' he agreed, surprised. A part of him had assumed that, if he yielded one more time, the matter would be settled. But now that they had been out twice without permanent harm, why not three times, or more? Now that he was married, it seemed like some type of social life was inevitable.

Emma gave a vast sigh of relief at his agreement and smiled at him from across the carriage.

At the sight of it, he felt another bit of the ice in his heart melting away. They were only a mile or so from home, too close to get into any real trouble, but far enough to give them time alone, together. He held his hand out to her.

She climbed across the carriage and settled into his lap to kiss him.

* * *

The next morning, Emma woke, smiling. Despite the incident at dinner, the evening had ended better than she'd ever hoped it would. Not only had Robert agreed to more outings, they had cuddled on the carriage ride home, passing the time with soft kisses and gentle caresses. She had been sad when they'd arrived at the house and he had sent her to bed alone. But it was a sweet melancholy compared to the cold loneliness of the first nights of her marriage.

She felt even better when she went downstairs and received a steady string of morning calls from the ladies who had not dared to speak to her on the previous evening, all wanting to hear the details of her daring rescue of Lord Fairfax.

She told them as best she could, not wanting to embellish the story, which was, in truth, a simple act of instinct on her part.

Each of them listened, wide-eyed, and declared it the most daring thing in the world and Emma the bravest woman they had ever met.

It was embarrassing, but in a far different

way than she was used to. She had been expecting a visit from her mother who would shame her for behaving outside the norm, yet again. But it was surprising to get such fulsome praise from others. And even more surprising that what she had feared would be a faux pas was resulting in more invitations as if the hostesses were eager to see what miracle she might perform next.

Hesitantly, she accepted. Though he had agreed to more outings last night, she was not sure her husband wanted her to make so many plans so soon. But the previous evening he had seemed as impressed as these ladies at her ability to handle a crisis. Perhaps he would trust her to do it again, should the occasion for dramatic action present itself.

When the tide of guests abated and Emma had shown the last of the ladies to the door, the butler stopped her to announce that she had one more visitor, still waiting.

'I do.' It was likely the expected visit from her mother. At least she would be able to assure her that the evening had not been the disaster that it appeared. If the past two hours were an indication, she was now a social success.

The butler presented a calling card on a silver salver and announced, 'Mrs John Gascoyne.'

'Robert's, I mean, our sister-in-law,' Emma said cautiously.

The butler's head inclined a fraction on an inch. 'She did not want to interrupt your other callers and is waiting in the green salon.'

It was an excellent choice if one wished to display the opulence of Gascoyne Manor. The room was named for the colour of the carved marble fireplace that dominated one wall. It was even better if one did not want to see or be seen by the master of the house for it was on the opposite end of the ground floor from his study. She hurried down the hall to greet her guest.

The butler announced Emma and the other lady turned to greet her, an embarrassed look upon her face. 'I hope you do not mind my arriving without invitation, Lady Gascoyne. But at least we managed to be introduced before I did it. If it weren't for the meeting at the festival, I fear our husbands would never allow us to meet at all. They do not get along, you know.'

'I was not aware of it until recently,' Emma said, reaching to take her hand. 'But I do not think that, whatever the problem is, it should matter between the two of us. Now that you have come, know you are as welcome in this house as you are in your own. Please, call me Emma.'

'And you must call me Lucy,' the other woman replied, staring around the room in wonder. 'Jack was raised here, but he never told me the house was so grand.'

Emma was surprised. 'You have never been here? But your family lives scant miles away.'

'We were never invited,' Lucy said, with a half-smile. 'His grandfather was as reclusive as Sir Robert is and must have been a tartar. Jack did not have the nerve to sneak us in and back then he was quite the most daring boy I'd ever met.'

'And his grandfather was the only one to live here, caring for a boy without help?' she asked.

'There was a series of governesses and tutors, but none of them stayed for long. While he still lived, their father remained in the city,' Lucy said, a cloud passing over her face. 'It was to be nearer the gaming hells. Even before, he had little time for his family if there was a game in play.'

'Robert mentioned something about a suicide,' Emma added cautiously.

'From what I have been able to gather, it happened shortly after the children were taken away,' she said.

Which led her to the question she really wanted to ask. 'And when they were young, did your husband notice any problems with his brother's health?'

Lucy gave a knowing nod. 'We heard of the difficulty he had after we had left the festival. Is he feeling more himself again?'

'Much better, thank you,' Emma replied, looking nervously in the direction of the hall. Though Robert seemed fine, she suspected he would not like to be the topic of conversation.

Lucy glanced to the door as well. 'When they were still in the care of their father, I was given to understand that they were often left alone in their rooms, without even a servant to see that they were fed and cared for. It was very hard on both the boys, but mostly so on Robert, who was older and felt responsible. The worry seemed to affect him physically.'

'How terrible,' she whispered, imagining the two small boys, hungry and alone, and Robert trying to solve the problem.

'But then their grandfather took them in and everything changed,' Lucy said with a sigh.

'He separated them,' Emma said. 'Robert was sent away to school and trained up to take the place of his grandfather.'

'Though they were thick as thieves at one time, Jack barely knows him any more.' Lucy's face darkened again. 'I understand from my husband that your husband can be a somewhat difficult man.'

'Difficult,' Emma said, puzzling over the word. 'I think complex would be a better word to describe him.' And confusing in ways that she did not want to discuss with a woman who was still a stranger to her.

'That gives me some hope,' the other woman said, 'that this estrangement between them is based on misunderstanding. I think he still views Jack as a child in need of protection.'

'Robert has said that he was very worried for Major Gascoyne's safety, when he was at war.' And now that she had seen what happened to him when he worried about others, she could imagine how difficult it had been for him.

Lucy seemed surprised at this. 'He tried to prevent Jack from going by denying him the money.'

Emma nodded, easily imagining Robert trying to rule over a grown man with dictums and ultimatums. Then, she asked, 'Has your husband spoken of a family curse or inherited bad luck?'

Lucy shook her head. 'He is prone to melancholy. But he has been far more likely to curse the good luck that kept him safe during the war and failed to protect his comrades. He has said nothing about problems in the family beyond the fact that the Gascoynes can be unreasonable and hard to deal with.'

'They both have their dark moods,' Emma said thoughtfully. 'And they care for the safety of others, more often then they think of themselves. I suspect that is why they have had trouble getting long. They are too much alike.'

'Possibly true,' Lucy said.

'And what would you say if we could get the two to reconcile?'

The other woman looked at her with wide eyes. 'I would think it a prodigious feat, should we accomplish it. But I think it would do my husband's heart good to believe that he had a brother living nearby and not a stranger.'

'And mine as well,' she said. 'Robert has been too much alone, these last years.'

There was the sound of footsteps in the hall, and Robert appeared in the doorway, his expression curiously blank. 'I did not know you were still entertaining visitors.'

Was that a warning that she had had too many morning callers? If so, she ignored it. 'Yes,' Emma said with what she hoped was an innocent smile. 'But only a member of the family.'

'Mrs Gascoyne,' he said, offering a deep and sombre bow.

Before he could question her presence there, Emma lied, 'After the delightful meeting at the festival, it only made sense to invite her to call on us.' She paused, waiting to see his reaction.

'Of course.' It seemed that he was not going to contradict her but it was clear, from the stiffness of his posture, that he wished to.

'Good morning, Sir Robert,' Lucy replied, not bothering to correct Emma's fib.

'We were discussing a gathering to celebrate our marriages,' Emma supplied quickly.

'Your mother's ball,' Robert replied, his frown deepening.

'I am sure she would enjoy it,' Emma agreed. 'But I was not planning it with her in mind.' Actually, she had not even considered something so elaborate as a ball. But now that her husband had mentioned it, it would be rude to retract the suggestion. She continued. 'With both Gascoyne brothers being married within months of each other, I see no reason why we should not do something to celebrate the unions.'

He raised an eyebrow. 'You can see no reason.'

'None that I would care to discuss,' she said, cutting her eyes to the woman next to her.

'We would be most honoured to be your guests,' her new friend said with a smile. 'But there will be much planning to be done before such a thing can happen.'

'It might take months,' Emma said, giving Robert a conciliatory look. 'It might not even be possible, this season. But perhaps you and Major Gascoyne can come to dinner tomorrow so we might discuss it.'

She did not have to look in the direction of her husband to know that he was angry. It was as if she could feel the heat rolling off him.

'That will be delightful,' Lucy said, rising to go. 'I will tell my husband of your plan and we will join you tomorrow.'

'And I shall search my social calendar for open dates,' Emma said, walking her to the door.

When she returned to the morning room, her husband was waiting there for her.

'You know my feelings on entertaining,' he said with a dark look.

'It is one thing to be against a major entertainment…'

'Like a ball,' he said.

'Which we have no firm plans for,' she added. 'But you have given me no specific prohibition about inviting family into the house for dinner. And I did not think you worried about suffering an attack in front of someone you have known your entire life.'

'You know that my brother and I do not get along,' he said.

'And how was I to know that?' she asked. 'You have been neighbours with your brother's wife's family for quite some time. But at the festival, you needed to be introduced to your own sister-in-law as if she was a stranger.'

'Because the festival was the first time I had seen her, since her marriage,' he said.

'Your brother did not come to get your blessing?' she said, surprised.

'It is not required that he do so,' Robert said. 'He is a grown man and not a child.'

'It is not a matter of obligation, it is a matter of affection,' she said, shaking her head.

'There was no time before the decision,

even if he'd wanted to tell me. His wedding was the result of an elopement,' Robert replied.

'And since?'

'I may have said something on our last meeting to make him think he was not welcome to return,' Robert said, his eyes refusing to meet hers.

'And what would that have been?' she asked.

'That I wished he would go to the devil,' Robert said, with the slightest of smiles on his face.

'What motivated you to say such a thing?'

'I believe it was his threat to black my eye.'

'So, you are both incorrigible,' she said, shaking her head in disbelief.

'That is one way to describe it,' he said.

'Well, then, what is to be done?' she said.

'Done?'

'I have promised his wife a ball,' she said. 'It will be most awkward if our husbands cannot be in the same room without fighting.'

'We do not actually fight,' he allowed. 'Of course, we are not usually together long enough for it to come to that.'

'Then the invitation to dinner was exactly what was needed. I suggest while they are here, we women will go off to the sitting room and the two of you drink your port and you will make an effort to behave in a civil fashion with your brother, as you do with me,' she reminded him. 'If he is all the relation you have and has survived Napoleon, despite your curse, he should be allowed to brave the family home without your attempts to drive him away.'

Chapter Sixteen

Emma was meddling in his affairs and he could not quite figure out what to do about it. Forbidding her from doing things was having surprisingly little effect.

Perhaps Jack had been right and marriage was softening him even after so little time. And thinking of that, what was he to do about the fact that she had invited his brother to dinner and expected them to get along as normal siblings did?

Under the lax care of their grandfather, his little brother had grown first into a reckless man, then into a decorated war hero. But Robert still remembered him as the frightened little boy who had been parted from him when they were young. Seeing him now was like meeting a stranger and being told to get on like family.

That was exactly what his wife was telling him to do. She should not be the one dictating to him. It should be his job to tell her what things were and were not done in this house. Yet he could not seem to manage it.

Most annoying of all, her efforts had, for the most part, been successful. Other than the unfortunate spell at the festival, the problems that had occurred had been minor enough that it made his refusal to socialise seem unnecessarily cautious. And when she had been faced with a real challenge at the Pritchett dinner, she had handled it with none of the panic he sometimes got when stressed.

Perhaps she truly was his better half. When he thought of her, he felt an unusual lightness of spirit, as if it might be possible to weather even the worst problems without fear. Such optimism was new to him and he was not sure he trusted it.

There was a cautious knock on the door and the butler entered and announced, 'Mr Watt is here to see you.'

It seemed he was about to get a chance to test his new mood. Watt was his man of business and a visit from him was never good news. Instinctively Robert braced himself for whatever fresh problem was about to be unveiled. 'Show him in.'

The man came into the room, taking a chair that Robert offered him. 'I have news on the mine in Cornwall,' his man of business said with no preamble.

'How could things get any worse than they already are?' Robert said, leaning back in his chair and waiting for the inevitable disappointment.

'I expected such a reaction from you. That was why I chose to deliver the information in person,' the other man said with a smile. Was there a hint of amusement in his voice, as if he was enjoying his chance to prolong the revelation?

There was that strange feeling of hope again, nagging at him that not everything had to be a disaster. Robert let out a puff of air and tried to pretend that Watt's delaying did not bother him. 'Very well then. You have news and you expect the worst from me. But you have yet to tell me what is going on.'

'The mine is running again,' Watt replied. 'They have found a fresh vein, even richer than the last one. Production has already begun and we can expect equally rich profits, just as we hoped from the first.'

Now, his mood changed from hope to shock at this unfamiliar turn of events. 'There is no chance that you have misunderstood?' he said, still not willing to believe what he had heard.

'I have just come from the mine and seen the ore myself,' Watt replied and now he was grinning.

'Very interesting,' Robert said cautiously, trying to understand what had been told to him. His luck always changed and no good news lasted for ever. But he could not remember the last time that bad luck had reversed itself. 'Please keep me abreast of any further changes.'

'Of course, Sir Robert.' Watt was still smiling at him, waiting to see shared enthusiasm. When it did not come, he excused himself with a promise to keep Robert informed of any changes, good or bad.

After he was gone, Robert sat in silence for a moment, stunned. If the mine paid as it should, that meant that he had not needed to marry in haste for money. He'd had but to be patient and wait for his investment to bear fruit.

But he could not seem to regret finding Emma. Though it had been impossible to get her to follow the rules he had set for her, he enjoyed the way she challenged him to be more than he had been. And mightn't it be possible that marrying her had caused the positive change in his fortune?

If that was true, he might be free of the fears that had plagued him for years. He had not been raised to believe that he would have a life where success was possible and death a thing that occurred at a ripe, old age. But suppose he had been wrong? What if all he'd ever needed was time, patience and someone who would argue him into optimism and force him to face his fears?

He grinned. If a dead mine could come back to life, then perhaps he could revive as well. But was he brave enough to test the limits of his luck?

He threw down the paper he had been reading and walked out of the house to the stable. Then, he had a groom saddle his most spirited horse. Titan was a large black gelding that he rode far too seldom, partly in caution from the risks that came with managing a big horse. But today the weather was fair and his spirits better than they had been in years. It was a perfect day to test his nerve.

He trotted away from the house, then brought the horse to a canter before turning and galloping for a fence at the bottom of the hill. It had been an age since he'd jumped even the smallest obstacle. Beth had still been alive and he'd been young enough to laugh at danger, certain that nothing could touch him.

Today, he must remember what it had felt like to be carefree and fearless. So, he took a breath and took the jump. The horse sailed over the obstacle as if there had been nothing in the way at all and he felt the all-too-brief feeling of weightless freedom, followed by the bump of landing.

He was whole and unhurt, as was the horse. There was not a trace of nervousness in him, nor any indication that he might be laid low by another attack. And for a moment, at least, he felt invincible. He felt even better as he turned them back towards the house and saw his wife, running to greet him, clapping her hands in glee. He stilled the horse so he could admire her movements, her long, graceful strides eating up the distance between them.

She arrived at his side flushed and out of breath, but still smiling as if seeing him was the greatest gift she could receive, and his heart clenched in a way that was entirely new, as if it was suddenly so full of feeling that it might overflow.

'Magnificent,' she said, staring up at him in wonder.

He grinned down at her and ran a hand through his windblown hair. 'Me, or the animal?' Then he tugged at his reins and brought his horse down into a bow.

She clapped her hands in approval. 'Both, of course. But your mount is a beauty.'

'You may pet him if you like,' he said, still smiling. 'He is surpassing gentle for an animal with such excellent spirit.'

Emma stepped forward and patted the velvety nose of the horse, only to have him snuffle in disappointment at her hand. 'No, I do not have a treat for you,' she laughed and whispered to the horse. 'But I will speak to your rider and see that you are well rewarded for your service.'

'There are several animals that would suit, if you are interested in joining me on my rides,' he said.

She stepped away hurriedly, shaking her head. 'Unfortunately, sir, I do not ride.'

'You do not ride,' he repeated, incredulous.

'Side saddles and I do not agree,' she said with a shudder that made him think of all the other ways she was hindered, trying to be a proper young lady.

Then, an idea came to him that he was sure would shock her, even though it was the most logical solution to her problem. 'Have you tried riding astride?' he asked.

'Of course not.' As he had expected, she sounded mortified at the very idea of it.

'As with so many other things we have discussed, you might find it will make your life easier if you do not try so hard to conform,' he said. 'Astride, you will have a more stable seat and I am sure you will find it easier to control the horse.'

She shook her head, adamant. 'I cannot ride astride in a skirt.'

'Then borrow a pair of my breeches,' he replied, thinking of how those long legs might look encased in buckskin. 'It is a most sensible garment for such activities.'

'I cannot dress like a man,' she said, 'Not even for the chance to…' She glanced back at the fence, clearly longing for a chance to take a jump.

'I could teach you to jump,' he said, daring her to misbehave. 'And to gallop. I bet you have never even tried that.'

'Of course not,' she said. 'The few times I went to Rotten Row we only walked the horses. Mother assured me that other gaits were not needed because I would surely break my neck if I tried them.'

'You will not be hurt if a skilled rider holds the reins,' he said and held out a hand to pull her up in the saddle.

She stared at his hand as if unsure of what to do.

'Let me take you up,' he coaxed. 'Just for a short ride around the yard. It is perfectly safe.'

She looked at him in amazement and well she should. He promised her safety. When had words such as those last left his mouth? But today, he was sure they were true.

'A short ride,' she said, as if today she was the one who needed convincing. Then she swallowed her trepidations and held out her hand to him.

He pulled her up easily and settled her in front of him, her hips pressing intimately into his breeches. A day ago, he would have put some distance between them to prevent temptation. But today, he feared nothing and hugged her all the tighter.

In response, she reached her hands timidly around his waist.

'That's it,' he said with a grin. 'Hang on tightly.' His elbows framed her body as he kicked the horse up to a trot.

'Oh, my.' He felt her trembling in his arms as the wind rushed by them, but it was from excitement rather than fear. So he nudged the horse to a gallop and made her squeal with delight. They tore down the road away from the house, the trees flying by in a blur on either side of them.

* * *

When they had gone nearly a mile, he drew the horse to a stop, his hands relaxing their grip on her and the reins. 'And what do you think of that?'

'Splendid,' she said, her eyes glowing with happiness.

'And if you were to ride astride, you might race me down the road on your own horse,' he suggested.

'It is wicked of you to even suggest it,' she reminded him.

'I am your husband,' he reminded her. 'I could command you to do it, if I wished.'

A thrill of heat passed between them at these words and he could not help imagining other things he might demand that had nothing to do with avoiding his bed.

'I have not been very successful at following your orders so far,' she reminded him with a smile.

'Then perhaps I should forbid you from riding, so you can do it to spite me,' he said.

She bit her lip, still considering. 'We would not leave the property. No one need ever know what I had done.'

'No one but me,' he said. And her maid and the groom that saddled the horses. Which meant that all the servants would likely know by supper time. But if she had not thought of that, he was not going to tell her.

'My mother would say that dressing like a man is most certainly wicked. And obviously it is unladylike.' Then she shrugged. 'But as long as she never knows, I will not have to hear the lecture. If it will make it possible for me to gallop without falling off the horse, I might be willing to try.'

'Very good,' he said, surprised at how much the prospect amused him. 'I will send a pair of breeches to your room and, the next time we go out, it shall be for a proper ride.'

Chapter Seventeen

For the dinner with her in-laws, Emma took extra care with the menu, sending a letter to Lucy to enquire if her husband had any favourite dishes that could be served. Thinking of her husband's warning about disastrous dinners of the past, she chose a fish course of poached pike that had been pulled out of the river that same day.

At eight, when her guests arrived, she greeted Lucy warmly and the other woman reciprocated, then stepped out of the way to reveal her husband, paused on the doorstep as if he had to push through some unseen barrier before he could enter.

Major Gascoyne was no longer in uniform, but he had the upright bearing of a military man and the keen eye of one used to watching for danger. Tonight, he was eyeing his old home as if he expected an attack might happen at any moment. Was he secretly obsessed with the curse as well? Or was it his brother that he did not trust? For he was staring at Robert as if at an enemy.

In turn, Robert stared back unsmiling, ignoring his brother's wife entirely and greeting him with the single word, 'John.'

'Robert.' Major Gascoyne's response was equally devoid of warmth. But as Robert stepped clear of the doorway, he entered, glancing around him in displeasure. 'The place has not changed since I was here as a child.'

'It has not been that long since I married,' Robert replied. 'It will take some time for Emma to shake the cobwebs from it.'

Was that what was expected of her? she wondered. Though she had instructed the servants to paint over the fresco in the ballroom, there had been no other talk of redecorating during any of the conversations she'd had with him. Perhaps it was a spiritual cleansing that was sought. At the moment, it certainly seemed like a dreary place, despite the tall ceilings and fine furnishings.

'It has been but six months since your own marriage, has it not?' Emma supplied, desperate to fill the void in the conversation.

'Boxing Day in Scotland,' Lucy supplied, her smile broad.

'It was very sudden,' Robert added in a way that bordered on rudeness.

'On the contrary, it was five years overdue,' the Major corrected, his face lighting up in a smile as he turned to look at his wife. 'I needed to find a way to make my fortune before I could be taken seriously as a suitor.'

'For my family, perhaps,' Lucy said with an equally fond look. 'I would have married you whenever you asked.'

'Now *your* marriage was sudden,' Jack said, changing the subject. 'Too quick to send out invitations to it, I gather.'

Emma winced, wondering if her mother had even bothered with a guest list, since she was so eager to see the two of them wed and a title secured.

'I did not think you would be interested in

coming,' Robert replied, his eyes locked on his brother's.

'We shall never know,' his brother reminded him.

'It is good that we live so near and have the opportunity to remedy that omission of hospitality,' Emma said hurriedly, glaring in her husband's direction. 'I hope dinner will be just as fine as our wedding breakfast was.'

'And it will give us the opportunity to speak without interruption of others in the party,' Lucy said, looking daggers at her husband as well.

'I am sure we have much to talk about,' Robert replied in a tone that said he had no idea what it might be.

As it turned out, the dinner was not as fine as the breakfast. Though the fish was excellent, the beef was burnt and the ice cream melted. Perhaps Robert had been right all along and they were cursed. On this, of all nights, she needed everything to go well, but could not seem to manage it.

At least the forced proximity of the two brothers allowed her an excuse to question them about the past to try to find some common ground between them. 'When was it that you first came to live here, Major Gascoyne?' she asked.

'I was all of seven at the time,' the Major said with a smile. 'Robert was twelve and sent away to finish his schooling.'

'And before that?' Emma probed.

'We were in the care of our loving father and stepmother,' Robert said with a roll of his eyes. 'I doubt Jack remembers much of the time we spent in London.'

'I was not an infant,' his brother snapped. 'I remember a series of indifferent nannies and tutors.'

'When they could afford them,' Robert added.

'And a certain permissive air to our free hours,' he added with a grin.

'That was how you remember it?' Robert said, his eyes wide with surprise.

'I remember you stealing food from the kitchen for us, and the odd feasts we would have, from whatever you could get away with,' Jack said with a grin.

'I gave you whatever food was left in the

house,' Robert said, sounding faintly disgusted. 'And when there was none to be found, I sometimes begged for scraps from the neighbours' servants.'

There was an awkward pause in the conversation. Then, Jack broke the tension with a nervous laugh. 'Well, I remember it as an adventure.'

'As you do almost everything about your life,' Robert snapped.

'It was one of my many character flaws that Grandfather tried to correct,' Jack said. 'That is how I ended up spending so much time with Lucy's family. To avoid the seemingly infinite rules of the household.'

'You could have considered following some of them,' Robert suggested.

At this, the Major laughed in earnest, as if the thought was far too ridiculous to take seriously.

'And we felt sorry for him,' Lucy replied with a grin. 'He was all alone in this great big house, with no playmates.'

'He'd have been better at school, with me,' Robert interrupted.

'This is the first time you have said so,' Jack said in surprise.

'Or perhaps not,' Robert corrected quickly. 'It was very difficult for me to catch up with the boys who had been properly educated. Many of my early lessons were beaten into me with the schoolmaster's cane.'

Emma paused, her fork halfway to her mouth. 'How horrible.' Given the childhood he'd had, it was a wonder that Robert had turned out as well as he did.

'Then it is just as well that I was not properly educated,' Jack said with a smile. 'I doubt regular beatings would have done me a bit of good.'

In response, Robert shrugged, as if that was exactly what he thought his brother had needed, then added, 'Of course, you, being younger, would have had an earlier start on lessons and might not have needed them.'

'If I'd have done any schoolwork,' Jack reminded him. 'When Grandfather bothered with a tutor, I was an indifferent student, at best. It was probably better for all of us that I ended up in the military.'

'It took years from my life, worrying about

you,' Robert said, in a strained tone. When Emma looked to him, there was a faint sheen of sweat on his upper lip and his breathing seemed shallow, as if he had to struggle to control it.

'What else was I to do with my life? There was no future for me in this house,' Jack growled in return. 'It was all to be left to you, who had not even lived here.'

Lucy shot Emma an alarmed look, as if to remind her that, since it had been her idea to get the two of them together, it was her job to keep them at peace.

'Tell me about your grandfather,' she said, to stop whatever was about to come next.

'He was a dictatorial old fool,' Jack said, without hesitation.

'He was a hard man who meant the best for us,' Robert responded.

'But did you like him?' Emma asked. 'Were you happier, once he took you away from your father?'

Apparently, the idea of warm emotion towards a family member was alien to them. For a moment, neither could manage to answer her. Then, Robert said, in a stiff tone,

'He did what he did out of duty. We could not have stayed where we were.'

'But it was cold comfort to some of us,' Jack said. Then he added, 'To those of us who did not know any better, at least.' Then, he looked to his brother with an expression that seemed to hold both exasperation and sympathy.

It was lost on Robert, who continued to stare into his plate as if the answers to all his problems might be written on it.

Emma gave an extra rattle of her dessert spoon to signify that the meal had ended, forced a brilliant smile and said, 'Let us retire to the sitting room and leave the gentlemen to their port.' She glared across the table at her husband to remind him that he was, indeed, expected to be a gentleman. 'I am sure they have much they want to say to each other.' Then, with a silent prayer, she led her sister-in-law from the room.

After the ladies left them, Robert and Jack retired to the library in silence.

It should not have surprised him that Jack had been unaware of how close they had come to starving. He had worked hard to keep the secret from him, at the time. But as it did each time they spoke, he was surprised by the conflicting emotions he felt when confronted with his brother's ignorance. The fear and the helplessness of childhood seemed to rush back, leaving him on the brink of another attack.

When that happened, it was far easier to lash out in anger and regain control, than to listen patiently to whatever it was his brother had to say to him.

To calm himself, he remembered Emma, laughing in the wind as he had galloped down the road with her. He must not think of things as they had been. He must remember that, maybe, just maybe, everything had changed for the better.

Even if they had, it was up to him to change the way things were at the moment. As there always was when the two of them were alone together, a heaviness filled the air, like the ominous feeling just before a storm. His brother must have sensed it, too, for he was watching Robert with a wary air as if he expected an argument to start the minute the door closed.

About this, at least, Emma had been right. The pair of them squabbled like children and it was no way for grown men to behave. But what was he to do to stop it? Would further conversations help it or make it worse?

As host, he must at least make an effort. He waved his brother to a chair in a way that he hoped was welcoming. But he suspected, from the look on Jack's face, that it was seen as the dismissive gesture of a lord to a servant, indicating that it did not matter what the other did as long as it was done quickly.

Inwardly, he winced, wondering what Emma would say of his awkwardness. Probably that he was making a simple thing far too complex. Judging by the look she had given him in the dining room, she would have no patience with failure.

'I do not think port is strong enough for the pair of us to converse politely,' Robert said in what he hoped was a light tone. 'But there is a fine brandy, if you are interested in a glass.'

Jack's brow furrowed for a moment, as if testing for a trap. Then, he shrugged. 'If it is the stuff Grandfather used to keep in his study, I might be persuaded to take a glass.'

'The same,' Robert supplied. 'And I suspect age has mellowed it since the last time you tasted it. It has been some years, has it not?'

'Since before the war,' Jack admitted.

'Then we should celebrate your return,' Robert said, pouring out two glasses. 'We have not done it as yet.'

At this Jack laughed. 'From your response the last time we spoke, I had no idea that you found my presence in England worthy of celebration.'

Honesty. That was what was required. Emma would make it all seem simple.

'If you felt I did not celebrate, you were mistaken,' he said. 'I was simply surprised at your return.'

'You lacked confidence in my abilities.'

'On the contrary. I did not trust fate, or your tempting of it. Our family has dashed bad luck, you know.'

'I had not noticed,' Jack said, as if years of trouble could roll from him like water off a duck.

'Not noticed...' This was surprising in

more ways than one. 'You were raised in this house, were you not? Did Grandfather never mention that we were cursed?'

'Grandfather blathered on about many things,' Jack replied and took a sip of his brandy. 'I believe, more accurately, he claimed to have been cursed with the presence of an extraneous child. He made it clear to me that, since I was not to inherit, I had best learn to appreciate what charity I was offered.'

'He called me an ignorant puppy and said he wanted no part of me until I had been properly trained up,' Robert said, remembering the continual berating he had received when he'd seen the old man. 'I assumed he preferred you, since he kept you instead of sending you away.'

'Preferred me?' Jack laughed. 'He threatened to thrash me whenever I came within arm's length. I spent as little time with him as possible. In turn, he allowed me to be raised by the neighbours.' Jack pointed a finger, the accusation in the gesture softened by the spirits they were drinking. 'He much preferred you. Or so he told me at each opportunity.'

'Did he now?' Robert said. 'He informed me that I was not worthy of his time or money, each time he saw me. He said that I was too stupid to be kin of his, since my marks were low and my schoolmasters despaired of my progress.'

'Then I suspect he did not like either one of us. Nor was he fond of Father for marrying three times without finding a woman who would last long enough to care for us.'

'Both Father and his wife were too busy at the faro table to care for children,' Robert agreed.

'True,' Jack replied. 'But I still wonder what they were about, letting us go without a word of objection. It always made me feel like failed horseflesh.'

'They were eager to get us off their hands before you died from their neglect,' Robert said, shaking his head in disgust.

'Died?' Jack replied, surprised. 'Surely things were not that bad at home.'

'You do not remember your frailty as a child,' Robert said, equally surprised. In his own memory Jack would always be a hollow-eyed child, unusually thin, who wheezed each time he took a breath.

'I remember feigning coughs when I realised that it would gain me a second biscuit at tea,' he said.

'Perhaps Grandfather kept you because we all thought you were not long for this world,' Robert replied. 'He told me once that the school would not allow you in because they were convinced that your weakness was a contagion.' It seemed he had not slept at all during those first months at school, worried that the next letter he received would inform him of the death of his brother.

'If malingering can be transferred, I suppose it was,' Jack said. 'Grandfather told me I was far too stupid to go to school.'

'Then my education was a waste,' Robert said, 'for he told me you were the clever one.'

Jack raised a toast to the fireplace. 'Further sign of what a disagreeable man he was. It is a shame we did not compare notes on him sooner,' he said.

'We might have listened to him less,' Robert agreed, trying not to think of the curse.

'Well, we do not have to listen to him any

longer,' Jack said, giving Robert a curious look. 'We are the only two left alive.'

'And the first thing I must do is to throw a ball to celebrate your marriage to Lucy, and your safe return from Waterloo,' he said, in a grim tone, feeling his throat tighten as another of the old barriers he'd erected began to fall away.

'You do not sound particularly excited by the idea,' Jack said, some of his wariness returning.

'It is my wife's idea,' he replied.

'If you do not wish to, then she needn't bother,' Jack replied, throwing back the last of his drink.

'It is your wife's wish as well,' Robert reminded him. 'And I assume you want to please her since she has done you much good. I have not seen you look so happy in years.'

'I have not been so happy since before the war,' he agreed. 'Lucy has done much to improve my mood, just as Emma has softened yours.'

This conversation was proof enough that she had changed him, in the short time they had been together. He would not have been capable of it, just a few weeks ago. 'She continues to amaze me,' he said, more to himself than to his brother.

At this, his brother gave him a knowing nod and held out his hands in a gesture of surrender. 'They are, indeed, amazing, but what are we to do with them?'

Jack sighed. 'I supposed it does not matter what we might prefer. If the women are decided, we will have to go along and make the best of it.'

'Says the old married man of half a year,' Robert said with a laugh.

Then Jack held out his glass in toast. 'Let us hope the surprises continue. To your wife and mine.'

'To our wives,' Robert agreed, since it seemed churlish not to. Then he added, 'Though I am still not sure that I like being surprised.'

'You will grow used to it, I'm sure,' Jack said. 'But until you have, do not seek a retreat to what you were if life is forcing you forward.' He held out his glass for a refill and they went to rejoin the ladies.

* * *

Later, after they had said goodbye to their guests, Robert walked his wife to her room. Once at the door, she looked up at him, eyes hopeful. 'The dinner was not as good as it could have been. But the rest of the evening went well, didn't it?'

'Yes, it did,' he agreed.

'And you were able to talk to your brother without arguing?'

'Yes,' he agreed again, giving her a frustrated smile. 'And I would not have tried to do so if it hadn't been for your interference.'

'Then will it be all right if I hold a ball?' she said, smiling at him expectantly.

'The two things have very little to do with each other,' he said, trying to ignore the way the scent of her perfume clouded his thoughts.

'There would not be one without the other,' she reminded him, taking a step closer to him.

He took a step back, trying to regain his resolve. 'I will consider it. Perhaps, if you come riding with me tomorrow morning, we might discuss it then.'

Now, she paused, obviously remembering

what they had discussed on their previous ride together. By the look on her face, she had agreed to his suggestion only to lose her nerve now that the time had come to implement it.

He walked down the hall and into his room, searching the wardrobe until he found a pair of leather riding breeches and a fresh shirt. They smelled of starch and horse instead of mind-boggling femininity. If he focused on that, perhaps he would be able to sleep without dreaming of her.

Then he returned and handed them to her. 'Meet me at seven in the stables, if you have the courage to do so. We will discuss your plans, afterwards.'

Chapter Eighteen

The next morning, as Emma prepared to meet her husband, she stared at the garments he'd given her, part in fascination and part in terror. She wanted to continue the discussion that he'd ended the night before and convince him that holding a ball would do no more harm than their other forays into society. He had only set this condition on it because he'd assumed she would refuse to meet it. She must prove him wrong.

But more importantly than that, she wanted to feel the freedom that she'd felt when riding with him on their last outing. If she wanted to gallop, it made sense to try an easier way than the genteel method everyone had attempted to teach her.

But wearing a garment that displayed the legs was simply not done. Did she ask her maid to help her with this improper activity or simply manage on her own?

She tried the shirt and discarded it, unsure of how she would hide the details of her body through the thin linen fabric. On attempting the breeches, she discovered that she did not need help to put them on, since the closures were, quite sensibly, in the front. But even when properly closed, the reflection in the mirror was so shocking that she dropped her skirts to hide them, then went to the wardrobe for a pelisse and closed it tightly to be sure everything was hidden.

Once she was sure she was decent, she made her way downstairs and out to meet her husband, but even walking in these strange clothes was difficult. She was not used to the feel of fabric between her legs and could not seem to decide where her feet were supposed to go. She had to resist the urge to swagger like a man and take long, bold strides that called attention to the change in attire. Instead, she forced herself to take small, ladylike steps as she walked further and further from the house.

When she arrived at the stables, Rob-

ert scanned her garments, obviously disappointed.

To prove to him that she had obeyed, she
timidly raised her hem all the way to the
knees, showing him the breeches underneath
her skirt.

He grinned. 'I suppose it was too much to
hope that you would wear them in plain view.'

'And show my legs as I walked from the
house?' she said, shocked. 'Since even you
have not seen them, I certainly do not want
to show the footmen.'

'You might be surprised at what I have already seen,' he said with a smug look, then
added, 'but you are probably right that I do
not want to share the view with the servants.
That is why I sent the grooms away, after they
saddled the horses.'

She had not noticed that they were alone,
but she was certainly grateful for it. Now her
husband was staring down at her skirts, expectantly. 'Why don't you tie that excess fabric out of the way so I can find your feet and
help you into the saddle?'

It made sense that she would not want to be
hindered by the skirts. It was the whole point

of wearing men's clothing. But now that the time had come to reveal it, she felt strangely hesitant. But this man was her husband and, above all things, she wanted him to notice her in the way a man noticed a woman. Perhaps this was a brazen way to go about it, but if there was a chance that it might work, she should try it.

She took a deep breath, closed her eyes and raised her skirts, bundling them at the waist and tying the hem into a knot to secure them.

When she opened her eyes again, her husband was staring down at her legs in silent fascination. Then he cleared his throat to hide his distraction, glanced up at her face and created a basket with his hands to take her foot and boost her into the saddle of a roan mare.

The act of throwing her leg over was unfamiliar, but she managed it without difficulty and smiled as she found herself seated securely on her mount's back and feeling more confident than she'd ever felt on a horse. She grinned down at Robert. 'Are you going to join me?'

Without another word, he mounted his

horse and they walked the horses out into the stable yard. The feeling of the animal moving beneath her was exhilarating and it grew even more exciting when she looked at her husband. Even at a walk, he rode his horse as if he had been born in the saddle, controlling it with the barest touch of the reins and a slight tightening of his legs.

She followed his lead, amazed at how quickly her mare responded to her every move. They rode down the path at an easy trot. When they reached the road, he pulled his horse to a stop and smiled across at her. 'Are you ready to run?'

She nodded, excited. Then, together, they dug in their heels and raced, laughing into the wind. When he slowed at a bend in the road, she passed him, then wheeled her horse around, coming to an uneasy stop beside him, triumphant.

When she looked at her husband, he was gazing back at her with pride and something else that was far warmer. 'Let us tie up the horses and rest for a few minutes,' he said, glancing towards a copse of trees at the side of the road.

She wanted to argue that she did not need to rest. But when she tried to dismount, her knees shook so that they could hardly support her. Before she could collapse, Robert was beside her, his arm in hers, supporting her as they walked into the trees. Once there, she leaned back into a stout oak, letting the trunk take her weight as she caught her breath.

'I knew you would take to riding,' he said, brushing a lock of hair from her face. 'Some women are good for nothing but drawing-room decoration. But you need to move.'

'And that is not unfeminine?' she said, surprised by his fervent tone.

'Believe me, my dear,' he said, 'I have no doubt that you are a woman.' He was staring down at her legs again and dropped a hand, almost casually, to caress her hip. Then he leaned forward and kissed her.

The length of his body rested against hers, pressing her back into the tree. And as his tongue slipped between her lips, she spread her legs and felt the bulge of his manhood, pressing gently, then harder, against her. Before he could change his mind, she wrapped her arms around his waist and circled her hips slowly against him.

He groaned into her mouth and his free hand slid between them, giving one of her breasts a possessive squeeze. His other hand was moving now, stroking her bottom, sliding down her legs and up between them, pressing her body against his. Then he stopped, but only long enough to reach for the fastenings of the breeches she wore. He undid them and thrust his hand inside to touch her.

What was happening was wicked, but she loved it. And if she gave him a moment to regain his sanity, it would all stop. So, she did as he had done and found the buttons at his waist, undoing them and fumbling her way inside.

He stiffened in shock when she touched him, then pulled away and whispered, 'You are driving me mad. But then, you have from the first. And do not dare to apologise for that.'

'I am not sorry in the least,' she said and her fingers brushed against his manhood. It was wonderful, dangerous, hard and yet velvety soft, and she felt her body throb as he stroked her in return.

His lips were on her throat, planting hard kisses at the base of her shoulder, nipping the skin, biting and sucking. She leaned her head back and stared up into the leaves above them, dazzled by the sunlight which seemed to grow brighter as he found her centre. Her body tightened, eager for something that she did not understand.

She pushed the fabric of his breeches aside to free him, nudging his hand out of the way and pressing the tip of him against her body. Then, instinctively, she bucked her hips and stroked him, encouraging him to do what they both wanted.

He hesitated for only a moment, before pushing forward. Then, he spread her with his fingers, leaving her trembling as he inched forward into her.

It was different than she'd expected, tight to the point of pain. Then he began to move. As her body adjusted to accept him she felt a wash of warmth and the first wave of pleasure. She wrapped her arms around him, burying her face against his chest, drinking in his scent and listening to the hammering beat of his heart against her ear.

She was finally his, body and soul, heart and heat. And, if she had not known it before, she was sure now. She loved him. The knowledge broke her and she cried out as he thrust, unable to control the joy spilling forth inside her. He followed her, shuddering and falling against her so that the tree behind them was the only thing keeping them from collapsing to the ground in a loving tangle of arms and legs.

When he could manage to catch his breath, he raised his head and looked at her, shocked. 'We should not have done that.'

She smiled back at him holding him even tighter so he could not withdraw. 'But we did.'

'But against a tree,' he said, shaking his head in amazement. 'I should have at least treated you with more respect.'

'I did not mind,' she said hurriedly.

He sighed in exasperation. 'That is not the point. I should have known better. I should have exercised restraint, just as I planned.' Then, he glanced down, towards her legs.

'But the sight of you in those garments… I lost all control.'

It was not quite as good as an announcement of love and devotion, but it was very flattering. 'Thank you,' she said and dipped her head to kiss his neck.

He groaned and she felt his body stirring inside her. 'I know I should tell you that it will never happen again, but I cannot seem to do so. Such things are quite hard to stop, once they have begun.'

She was not sure that she liked him describing the act of love between them as a *thing.* That made it sound as though it was not the profound revelation she had had. But she must comfort herself with the fact that he was having trouble resisting it. 'Good,' she said. 'Because I do not want to stop.'

'You still do not understand how dangerous this could be for you,' he said.

'It does not have to be,' she said, giving a gentle nudge with her hips to distract him. 'You are worried about the possibility of children, are you not?'

'And I am as adamant as ever on that subject,' he said. 'I do not care if the curse seems to have abated. I will not take risks with your life.'

If he no longer believed he was cursed, it explained the chances he was taking on his horse and with her, just now. She must hope that time would further weaken his resolve. 'There are things we can do to prevent a child,' she reminded him.

'To begin with, I must be far more careful than I was today. I should not have allowed myself release.'

Remembering how wild he had been at the end, she wondered if such control had even been possible. 'But if we were very careful from now on?' she prompted.

'Then we could do more of what we have just done,' he said, smiling as if he would like nothing better.

She nodded enthusiastically.

'We must go back to the house and discuss this further,' he said.

'In our bedchambers, I think,' she said with a grin.

'Let us go to the horses and I will race you home,' he replied.

* * *

Robert spurred his horse towards the stables, every nerve aware of the woman who rose at his side. Never in his life had he forgotten himself so completely. When one did not want children, one didn't engage in congress with a woman. If one was careless enough to attempt it, then one practised withdrawal before the completion of the act. One did not indulge every desire and lose oneself in kisses, or in a lush body ready for his entry.

He had known these things. But then he had seen her legs. He had thought that suggesting she wear breeches to ride had been a daring but sensible suggestion and that masculine clothing would diminish her charms instead of increasing them. In that, he had overestimated his control. Well-turned ankles, shapely calves and long thighs had been his undoing. Even now, the thought made him shudder with desire and a boyish eagerness to do the whole thing again when they got back to the house.

But it had still been an unforgivable risk to love her to completion. He must trust that, this time, they would be lucky and nothing would come of it.

The idea of trusting to luck made him want to laugh. Until recently, he had not considered that luck might be anything other than bad. When he was with Emma, he could believe anything was possible, even good fortune, but he must be careful. He had experienced a similar optimism when he'd been with Elizabeth, only to have it dashed.

But he did not remember this driving need to be with his first wife that he felt when he was with Emma. Perhaps it was the weeks of denial that had sharpened his desire for her. But now that he had failed in his original plan, he did not want to go back to it. Was it really so terrible to want what other men were allowed and have an ordinary marriage?

It would be if Emma died because of him. In the future, he would be careful, just as he had promised her, and make sure that he did not spill his seed inside her. There must be no children. The records in the family bible were undeniable. Gascoyne brides did not survive to see their children. It was one thing to believe that the curse might be ending and quite another to risk the very reason it had ended. Now that he had found her, he could not lose her.

They had reached the stables and he helped her down from the horse and untied her skirts so they fell to hide the unladylike garments that had been his undoing. Then she seemed to stumble deliberately, so he could catch her, pulling her into his arms and losing himself for a moment in another perfect kiss.

When he released her, her eyes sparkled with mischief. 'Now, are you willing to discuss the ball? Or must it wait until we are in the bedroom?'

He laughed. 'Are you thinking to hold me hostage at the moment when I can deny you nothing?' Then he held up his hands in surrender. 'Do not bother. You and Lucy can have your ball. I must trust by now that you are capable of handling any troubles that may occur because of it.'

'There will be no troubles,' she said hurriedly. 'I assure you, all shall be fine.'

To his surprise, he believed her. Without wanting to, he had been expecting some of the usual signs of impending disaster that he felt when she pressed him to do things he avoided. But today, his hands were warm and his breathing clear. And when he looked at her his usual dark mood evaporated and he felt nothing but optimism.

He reached down and took her hand, raising it to his lips, and agreed. 'Everything shall be fine, as long as you are here to see to it.' And that was why he must remember to keep her safe.

Chapter Nineteen

As Robert stood in the doorway of the cleaned and renovated ballroom, he had to admit that it looked a hundred times better than it had when he'd used it as a tennis court. The chandeliers had been brought down and cleaned, the marble floors buffed and polished so not a single boot scuff remained on them and the horrible fresco had been scraped from the wall and painted over in unassuming sage green to match the curtains that had been hung over the freshly washed windows.

The only thing missing now was the guests.

Thanks to Emma, in less than a week's time the room would be full of friends and neighbours, celebrating the marriage he had not known he'd needed. Once again, he tested his mood on the idea and was surprised to find he was both calm and, if truth be told, a little eager to see his brother again. Was it possible that he was actually looking forward to something he had denied himself for ages?

He might say the same thing for his relationship with his wife. Now that they were intimate, he could hardly remember why it was that he had wanted to deny himself. As long as they were careful, there was no reason why they could not continue as they were doing for a full and happy lifetime.

In fact, the release of sexual energy had done him good. Since he had been with her, his nerves had been rock steady, his mind untroubled and there had been no hint of panic or elevated heart rate. Perhaps the act of love was all that he had needed.

He glanced out into the corridor and saw her approaching, a hesitant smile on her face as she noticed where he was.

He grinned back at her. 'I was just admiring the servants' work. They have done well, as have you.'

'I am glad you approve,' she said, relaxing a little. But, surprisingly, she surveyed the room with a frown rather than a smile.

'And does it make you happy?' he asked.

'Women are supposed to like entertaining and entertainments in all forms,' she said, forcing herself to look happier, though she sounded rather glum at the prospect. 'And I know you assumed from the first that I would be eager to throw a ball.'

'But you were not?' he said, surprised.

'It is more from obligation that anything else,' she said. 'It is the right thing to do for your brother and his wife. But I am unsure of how I will do as a hostess since I do not make the best of guests. It is the dancing, you see,' she said with finality.

'What about it?'

'I am not very good at it,' she admitted. 'All those little steps and my too-long legs do not match up.'

'It is difficult being the tallest man in the set as well,' he agreed. 'Constantly having to correct my steps for the deficiencies of the people around me.'

'If you were a woman, you would learn to view the situation not as a lack from others, but as an unfortunate excess on your part,' she reminded him.

It was a shame to see she still had concerns

about her awkwardness, for as her confidence had grown, she had been doing quite well at avoiding the minor accidents that had marked the early days of their marriage. But if they had to have one, he wanted the ball to go well as much as she did. He contemplated the situation for a moment. 'Is it all dances that you have difficulty with, or just the line dances?'

'Those are the only ones I have been allowed,' she said.

He held out his arms to her. 'Then, I suggest we try a waltz. It is a simple dance and we are fairly matched in height. I suspect you will find it much easier.'

She stepped into the circle of his arms.

'The step is easy. One, two, three. And I will show you where to go like so.' He gave a gentle push with his palm and spun her once around. 'Are you ready?'

She nodded. Then she moved as he led her. As with other activities, he was surprised at how quickly she could learn. With no one else in the room, Robert made no effort to contain his movement, circling the room in long easy strides and wide looping turns. In no time, they'd arrived back at the point where they had started and he released her. 'You can dance,' he said with a definitive nod. 'It was just a matter of finding the right one.' Then he pulled her even closer so he could kiss her.

As her belly touched his, she pulled away. It was a surprise that she would want to keep a chaste distance between them, for she'd showed no such shyness in the bedroom, only a few hours before.

'What is the matter?' He laughed, then looked at her with concern. Though she usually had as much or more energy than he did for games of all kinds, it appeared she had been winded by the activity. 'Are you well?'

'Overtired,' she said hurriedly. 'Nothing more.'

'Then you must go to your room, and rest,' he said, smiling fondly. 'You have been working too hard and you want to be at your best for the guests.'

'Of course,' she said, backing away from him. 'I will do just that.' Then, she rushed from the room, her hand over her mouth.

She had been sick, again.

It was the third time in a week that Emma

had cast up her breakfast, even though she'd had nothing more than dry toast and weak tea. All the more maddening was the utter lack of normal sympathy from her maid, Molly, who grinned at her as if each succeeding accident was a blessing.

Robert, however, was more than sympathetic enough for both of them. When he'd realised that she was ill, he'd followed her to her room, asking through the closed door if there was anything he could do.

She had assured him, in a shaky voice, that it was a minor upset. She would be fine, given time and rest, just as he had recommended.

Once he had gone, she counted on her fingers, trying to remember the date of her last courses which had come some weeks before the day that her husband had taught her to gallop and to love. Since then, they had been careful, just as her husband wanted them to be. Between them, they'd discovered a wide variety of pleasures that minimised the risks of having children. Though he had relented in all his other prohibitions, he was just as adamant as ever that they remain childless.

But on that first time, there had been no

such care taken. He had spilled his seed inside her, just as nature had intended. When her mother had explained the way such things worked, she had warned Emma that her honour was precious because one mistake might be all it would take to become pregnant. Apparently, that was the truth.

Now, as if guessing what she had been trying to remember, her maid gave her another sly smile. 'Five weeks late.'

She had been so busy preparing for the ball, she had not thought of it. Of course, she had also been busy doing the very thing that was the cause of her current predicament.

She had not wanted to worry about such things because she had not wanted to spoil how nearly perfect her marriage had become. Her husband had yet to announce that he loved her, but he made it clear each night that he wanted and desired her. And it had been some weeks since he had even mentioned the curse that had worried him so much when they'd first married. But the news she had for him was likely to change everything.

'Do I need to call a doctor?' she asked, hoping that there might be some chance she was wrong.

The maid shook her head. 'There is nothing for them to do for quite some time. Some would say there is little for them to do at the last. These matters usually take care of themselves if they are left to progress naturally.'

She nodded, suspecting that what Molly said was true, but still feeling quite overwhelmed by the truth of her situation. Suppose she was wrong? Suppose what had started by accident ended in a miscarriage as these things sometimes did? Was it even necessary to tell Robert until she was sure?

And what was to be done with his weird superstition about the fate of the Gascoyne brides? Things had been going so well between them. But now, what should be the happiest of truths was likely to change everything. He had requested after the interlude on their ride that, if she thought she might be breeding, she tell him of it immediately. But what did he mean to do with the knowledge?

The thought brought yet another new fear. Her mother had also told her that there were certain herbs that put an end to such things, if they were done early enough. Would he be so callous as to suggest that she take them, if she came to him with her news?

That must not happen under any circumstances. Now that she had settled successfully into the role of wife, she was not nearly as afraid as she had been of becoming a mother. She wanted this baby, his baby, growing inside her. She wanted more than just a marriage, she wanted a family.

Just as much, she wanted to prove to her husband that there was no merit in his fear that she was doomed to die. They would never be truly free until he had given up the last vestiges of his superstition. She knew she would be strong enough to bear him a child. She must find a way to make him believe it as well.

But that might take time. It seemed the best way to manage the situation was to allow him his moods, gently encourage him to the truth and deny him knowledge that might affect her until it was too late to do anything but carry through with the pregnancy.

'How long until others are aware of my condition?' she asked Molly, who seemed to know more on the subject than she had ever learned.

'Some months, I think. It is different, one woman to another. But you are…' Molly paused, trying to find a polite way to say it, then didn't bother. 'You are a large woman and the baby is small. You might go five months with no change other than a loosening of the stays.'

'That is good to know,' she said, with a sigh of relief. 'And you will not tell anyone, do you understand?'

'Yes, my lady.'

'Not a single other servant. And certainly not the master.'

'Yes, my lady.'

Now, there was nothing to do but trust that the secret could be kept until she could find a way to tell her husband the truth.

Chapter Twenty

When Emma finished breakfast the next morning, the butler announced that her mother was waiting for her in the receiving room. She went to her and could see the reason for the visit, even before her mother began to speak. Her invitation to the Gascoyne ball was clutched in her hand and she was tapping it nervously against her knee. Emma had been assuming this moment would come and was no more eager for this than she was to explain her condition to her husband.

'Mother,' she said, doing her best to offer a welcoming smile that did not betray her panic. 'I see you have received the post. Have you come to accept in person?'

'I have come to ask the meaning of this,' she said, waving the paper in front of Emma's face.

'I thought you would be pleased,' she said, pretending to be surprised. 'After all, I am doing just as you wished me to do. We are having a celebration for Robert's brother and of course you are invited to it.'

'And how do you expect to plan such a major gathering without my help?' her mother snapped. 'You know you are not up to the challenge, Emma.'

For a moment, Emma believed her. Then she remembered that most of the work had already been done. 'Things have gone well, so far,' she said. 'And I have the help of Mrs Gascoyne, should I need it.' But it had surprised her at how little help she had needed. 'It is really coming together quite well.'

'Let me see the guest list,' her mother said, fluttering like an angry hen. 'Let me see the menu.'

'No.' Emma had not realised how little she had used the word until it was out of her mouth. But apparently it was rare enough to send a shock through her mother and a thrill of independence through Emma. So, she repeated it. 'No, Mother. I am quite capable of organising this without your help.'

'But I had thought—' her mother said.

Emma interrupted her. 'You had thought to run my life as you did before I was married. But I am a wife now, Mama, and not just a daughter. I must learn to think for myself.'

For a moment, her mother's jaw flapped like a gasping fish. She was not used to being refused by anyone, nor did she like being interrupted. She had never before accepted either of those things from her daughter. 'You cannot talk to me that way,' she said at last, too shocked to be angry.

'I just did,' Emma replied, amazed with herself. 'And although I would prefer not to do it again, I shall if I need to.'

'That doesn't mean I have to listen to it,' her mother said, standing up to go.

'Does that mean that you will not be coming to the ball?' Emma asked, her eyes wide and innocent.

This stunned her mother to silence, yet again. As upset as she was with Emma's rebellion, she would not respond to it by forfeiting an invitation to the social event of the year. She sank slowly back into her chair. 'I am sorry if you think that I am trying to rule your life. It was never my intent.'

That was probably true. Emma doubted that her mother had given so much thought to her behaviour as to intend the harm she created. Today's admission was not quite a real apology, so it was rather hard to give a real acceptance. 'I understand,' Emma replied, for those words seemed to suit better than any.

'And even if you do not want my help with the ball, you are going to need me sooner rather than later,' her mother said, as a smile dawned on her face.

'What do you mean?' Emma said, afraid that she already knew the answer.

Her mother gestured to her waist. 'My dear, you are *enceinte*. Surely you knew.'

'Mother,' she said, struggling to think of what to say next.

Her mother put her hands on her cheeks, her mouth forming in an O of surprise. 'But it is still a secret.'

Emma nodded, relieved. 'I am waiting until I am sure.'

'Then I shall not tell a soul,' her mother said, rising to go and taking her hands. 'And

I promise, from now on, I shall not meddle until you ask me to.'

'Of course not, Mother,' Emma said with a smile, knowing that the promise was well intentioned, but would not be kept. But now that she had managed to refuse her mother's help for the first time, it would become easier to do it again.

The night of the ball arrived and the house began to fill with people. It was not enough that it was the first big gathering of her life— if it did not go perfectly, it might be her last chance to entertain. If even the smallest thing went wrong, it might upset Robert to the point of having an attack. Then he might close the doors of the house for ever.

Or perhaps not. When she looked to him, he seemed calmer than he ever had and far more at ease over the event than she was. Of course, he did not have a secret to keep, as she did, nor was he experiencing the drain in energy that came with nurturing a new life.

Perhaps her maid thought it would be possible to hide a pregnancy for months on end, but Emma doubted she could manage it for much longer. Her mother had guessed it in a single glance and Robert had already noticed her fatigue and her occasional illness. In time, he would guess the reason for it. It would be better for all concerned if she explained herself before he figured it out on his own.

But for the moment, she must put all that behind her and focus on the evening. As guests of honour, Major Gascoyne and Lucy were the first to arrive. The Major surveyed the room with a critical eye and looked at her with faint surprise. 'You have had the room repainted, I see.'

'Do you approve?' she asked, holding her breath.

He nodded, then looked to his wife, Lucy. 'There was the most ghastly mural imaginable on the far wall. Cherubs dancing in a glade. Grandfather caught me bouncing a ball against it and caned me.'

'Your brother was using it for tennis practice,' she said, not bothering to disguise her smile.

At this, he looked amazed. 'Robert did something like that?'

'As recently as last month,' she assured him. 'You will be pleased to know we are reopening the tennis court.'

'Now that I have someone to play with, I have no reason to volley against a wall,' Robert said, stepping forward to join them.

'You were always good at sports,' his brother said, as if it took effort to dredge up the memory from childhood.

'And Emma has been a worthy opponent for any game I have chosen,' Robert said with pride. 'She is a good dancer as well.'

'I am not,' she insisted, blushing at the thought of leading off the first dance. But she needn't have worried for he had made sure that it would be a waltz and they circled the floor together as if they had been born for each other's arms.

Things were going well, but Emma could not ignore the seed of doubt that the evening would be a disaster in some way. She was not precisely expecting a problem, but she had gone out of her way to guard against it. She had called for more food than it was possible to eat. There was enough wine to drown an admiral.

Her parents were embarrassing, talking freely to all the guests and careless of rank and proper introduction. But that was hardly a surprise, nor was it something she could prevent. She had but to endure it, as she had so many other interactions with them.

Beyond that, the guests seemed to be having a pleasant time and gushed to her that they were pleased to have been invited. The honoured couple were happy as well. Lucy was a light-spirited girl who stood up for almost every dance. Major Gascoyne was in an excellent mood, smiling more often than she had seen him do in their previous interactions and dancing almost as much as his wife did.

It was then that a pigeon flew in through one of the open windows.

If she wished to think as Robert had done, she would have noted that birds were usually asleep at that hour and not fluttering around the terrace begging for crumbs. She might have remarked that it would be far more likely to have scared up a bat. She could blame the Gascoyne family curse for this ill omen.

Or she could simply think as she always did and put it down to the fact that Emma Harris could change her name and her social set, but that did not mean she was gifted in the art of social grace. That explained what happened next.

The bird made a few lazy circles around the room, swooping low over the guests and eliciting screams from some of the younger ladies, who covered their hair with their hands, as it passed, to protect against accidents.

The footmen ran to get brooms. Some of the more inebriated gentleman stripped out of their evening coats and swung them at the bird, which escaped them easily.

It was then that Emma decided she had to do something herself. Even as a voice inside her cried out that she was better off leaving the matter to the men, she could not help but notice that the men were not accomplishing very much. Worse yet, the bird was heading towards the buffet and she did not want it to ruin the food.

So, she removed a slipper, took aim and hit the pigeon in mid-flight. The bird was stunned and dropped, along with the shoe, into the silver punchbowl at the end of the table.

There was a moment of shocked silence, then several things happened at once. The footman manning the punchbowl scooped the bird and shoe out of the liquor and wrapped them both in a towel, hurrying for the nearest exit. Another grabbed the bowl and headed in the opposite direction, towards the kitchen.

On the other side of the room, her mother let out a shriek of horror at her daughter's latest social disaster, fell into a swoon and required hartshorn, furious fanning and several glasses of ratafia before she was in any condition to withdraw from the room.

And Sir Robert Gascoyne and his brother the Major burst into simultaneous and unrestrained laughter.

'The evening was memorable,' Robert said, after the guests were gone and they were walking to their rooms.

'If by memorable, you mean disastrous,' she said, closing her eyes against a vision of a wet pigeon begin carried from the ballroom.

'I have some experience with disaster,' he

said in a mild tone. 'Believe me, this was not as bad as I always feared it would be. You can console yourself that even I would not call it a cursed evening.'

'That is because you were not the one who threw their shoe in the punchbowl,' she replied.

'That was an impressive shot, by the way,' he replied. 'My brother agreed that neither of us could bring down a bird on the wing like that.'

'I am glad you could find common ground,' she said, annoyed. 'But I would be even more happy if it would have been on any subject other than my public embarrassment.'

He put an arm around her and pulled her close, kissing her lightly on the cheek. 'You will likely find that the post is full of thank-you notes, proclaiming it the event of the season. Even those who were not invited will be eager to have us as guests.'

'Because they want to see what outlandish thing I will do next,' she said with a moan.

'Evenings with you are never dull,' he agreed. 'But that does not mean they will invite you just to gawk. I heard several ladies call you refreshing and that was after the incident with the pigeon.'

'Refreshing,' she repeated. 'I am still not sure it is a compliment, but I suppose it will have to do.'

They were standing in front of his door now and she placed a hand on his as he turned to open it.

He smiled at her. 'Are you waiting for an invitation?'

'Are you willing to offer one?' she responded.

'Will this do?' He leaned down to kiss her then, slowly, thoroughly, his tongue matching the dart and flutter of hers. Then he opened her door and pushed her through it. 'You did wonderfully.' His hand stroked her back until he found the closures of her gown.

'And now do you believe that it is safe to entertain?'

'Do you believe that you are a successful hostess?' he asked.

She flinched.

'Let us not discuss such things now,' he said, leaning in for another kiss and tracing the neckline of her bodice with his finger.

He bit the side of her throat. 'In fact, I do not want to talk at all.'

She reached up and tugged at his cravat. 'Neither do I.'

They left a trail of his clothing from the door to the bed, as she stripped him, running her hands over his bare chest and kissing him open-mouthed while he fumbled with the buttons on his breeches.

He struggled free of them and sat down on the bed, pulling her, still fully dressed, on to his lap. Her skirts billowed about his legs and she felt the touch of his hand and the slide of his member into her body. There was a pause, then, as the two of them adjusted to the contact. Then he reached behind her and undid her gown and stays, pushing her clothing over her head and away, until she was as naked as he was.

Their coupling was quick and frenzied, over almost as quickly as it had begun. As usual, he withdrew before he was finished, so that he could finish alone.

She would have to tell him soon, she thought, noticing the beginnings of a bulge

on her normally flat stomach. But not tonight.
At the thought, she shivered nervously.

'Cold?' he asked, reaching for a blanket.

She nodded.

'The chimneys in this house do not draw
properly,' he said. 'Surely you have noticed
the fact.'

'On the contrary, my room is delightfully
warm,' she said.

He looked surprised. 'My room has always
been cold, even in summer. So has my study.'

'And are they both in the same corner of
the house?' she said.

'One is beneath the other,' he admitted. 'On
the north-east corner of the house.'

'Then your problem is with the single chimney on this side of the house,' she said.

He looked at her, surprised. 'I always assumed…'

'That it was the fault of your luck,' she finished his sentence for him. 'You probably
felt even more depressed because you were
cold. But it is a situation that is easily reme-
died. If you cannot fix the chimney, then you
should move your rooms to the other side of
the house.'

'My room has always been on this side of the house,' he said, confused.

'Then suit yourself. But do not blame a family curse for something that is your own stubborn unwillingness to change.'

'I am not stubborn,' he said, but the jut of his jaw said otherwise.

'Of course not, darling,' she said, stretching her feet to tangle with his. 'But you are cold. Next time, we will go to my bed, which is warmer.'

Suddenly, there was a pounding on the door.

Robert threw the blanket over her and grabbed for his dressing robe. 'What the devil is anyone doing, interrupting us at this hour?'

'Sir Robert?' The butler's voice was subdued as befitting the time, though it lost none of its urgency. 'There has been carriage accident. It is the Major.'

For a second Robert froze, as the information registered in his mind. Then his face went deathly white and his hands trembled as he called for his valet and began fishing through the clothing he'd so hastily removed a few moments before.

'What are you doing?' she said, watching as he paused to grip the back of a chair as if overcome by a sudden wave of weakness.

'I am going to help,' he said.

She tried to remember what he had looked like, just before the spell at the festival. That time it had seemed that one minute he was normal, the next he could barely stand. And now, after weeks of peace, it was happening again. 'You are in no condition…'

He turned and gave her a quelling look, then tossed her ballgown in her direction. 'I will be the judge of that. Now, cover yourself before Jenks gets here.'

She nodded, eyes wide.

Before she could offer any useless platitudes, he said, 'I have no idea why I let you talk me into throwing a ball.'

'You cannot blame—' she said.

'You?' he asked.

'A curse,' she corrected.

'When what has happened before happened again, in just the same way?'

'We do not know that,' she said. 'We only know that it was a carriage accident.'

'That happened to the guests of honour,' he replied.

'A coincidence. Nothing more than that,' she said.

'How glib of you to say such a thing when it is my brother's life that may hang in the balance.'

It was some comfort to know that he cared deeply for his brother, even if he was unable to show it, for he was truly distraught, his hands shaking as he slipped into his coat. 'I will go and see to him. You—' he pointed a dire finger in her direction '—go back to your room.'

Perhaps it was the pregnancy that made her moody. Or perhaps it was because his fit of temper had come so soon after a night of compliments and lovemaking. His sudden anger hurt more deeply than anything he had said to her. But she might push him into another attack if she gave way to her emotions now. So she took a calming breath and said, 'Send word when you know the truth of the matter', gathered her clothes and returned to her room to cry in private.

Chapter Twenty-One

It had been too good to last.

Nearly two months had gone by without a single disaster he could attribute to the family curse and no sign of a nervous attack. He'd truly begun to believe that Emma had been set free.

But now he was struggling through the worst spell in ages and could not afford the luxury of a collapse. Jenks, the valet, argued, just as his wife had, that he was in no condition to go out and that he must let the servants deal with whatever had happened.

Robert shrugged off the man's concern, trying to ignore his racing heart. He needed deep breaths and brandy. Brandy, at least, since he could not manage the other for himself without the help of a sedative. He demanded a drink, refusing the laudanum that Jenks offered to go with it, and felt steady enough to go down the stairs and out to the stables.

The walk gave him a chance to find some composure. He was probably overwrought for nothing. It did not seem fair that his brother, who had survived the worst Napoleon could give him, might be ended by accident a few miles from home.

But then he remembered there was nothing fair or rational about the Gascoyne luck. The thought hit him so hard that he pitched out of his saddle when he tried to mount his horse.

The grooms persuaded him that it would be more useful and perhaps safer for him if he took a dray. But it was nearing dawn by the time Robert was able to get the wagon harnessed and proceed to the site of the accident.

By the time he arrived, the injured had been ferried back to Jack's home for care. He was assured that these consisted of a coachman with a dislocated shoulder and a tiger with a bump on the head. Mrs Gascoyne was shaken, but unhurt, as was the Major. The carriage itself had broken an axle and was tilting wildly into the ditch. The horses had been unharnessed and led away, uninjured.

It was not, perhaps, as dire as it first sounded. But he would not know until he had seen Jack for himself. So, for the first time in his life, he sent the servants home with the dray and walked the few miles to his brother's house to discover the truth.

The home was large, clean and modern, one of many new manors that had been built in the area in the last decade from land that had once belonged to the Gascoyne family. When he arrived, the servants were already up, but his brother and wife were still in bed, recovering from the harrowing ride home.

Since the butler refused to wake Jack, Robert took a seat in the library and announced he would wait as long as necessary, until he had been assured of his brother's health. He requested a bottle of brandy and to be left to his own devices until such time as the Major woke.

Only then did he allow himself to fall apart. He gritted his teeth and pressed a numb hand over his chest, for it sometimes felt that he needed to hold his heart in place to keep it from beating its way out of his ribs. Logic told him he would not really die, only because he never had before.

Perhaps, this time, he might. Jack would come down to find him cold and stiff with no explanation of why he had come here in the first place. It was a shame. They were doing better, the two of them. But there was still much he had not said that his little brother deserved to hear.

For a moment, he succumbed to despair and the terror washed over him, blotting out common sense, leaving nothing but the conviction that this was to be the end for him. He had left Emma with words of anger that he could never retract, blaming her for his own weakness and his dread of what was happening right now. He had lived as a coward and now, he would die as one. He closed his eyes and waited for the end.

But eventually, just as the feelings always had, they began to ease. The clock on the mantel said it had been less than a half an hour since he'd sat down, but it had felt like an eternity and he was left drained, barely able to lift the glass that his brother's butler had left for him. He closed his eyes and spent the next hours in an uneasy sleep, waiting for Jack.

It was nearly noon when that man made an appearance, tired, but otherwise no worse for wear. He took one look at Robert, stretched out in a chair by the fire, and yawned. 'What the devil are you doing here?'

'I came to see if you had survived the crash,' he replied, feeling somewhat embarrassed in the full light of day.

'How dramatic of you,' Jack replied, laughing. Then his expression changed. 'From the tone you use, I could almost believe you are serious.'

'I am completely serious. Are you wounded in any way?' he said. It was still possible for even the smallest scratch to turn septic and what a cruel joke that would be.

'Certainly not,' Jack said, with a huff. 'I am a bit bruised from trying to help unhitch a frightened horse. But I do not mean to drop my breeches and show you where I was kicked.'

'The last ball that was held in that ballroom

ended in the deaths of the couple it was held for,' Robert informed him.

'And you thought history was going to repeat itself?' Jack said, with a look far more sceptical than any that Emma had given him.

'The thought had occurred to me,' Robert replied.

'Well, it did not. I am fine. And since you have not yet asked, Lucy was totally undamaged by the accident as well.'

'Of course,' Robert said hurriedly. Then added, 'But Lucy is your responsibility, not mine.'

'You speak as if you have a responsibility for me,' he said, with another laugh. Then he looked at him, surprised. 'That is what you think, isn't it?'

'Our father's last words to me were that I take care of you,' he said with an embarrassed shrug. And he had failed dismally at it.

'That was when I was a boy of seven,' Jack replied. 'But I have not needed a guardian for a very long time and I have not listened to one for even longer than that.'

'I am well aware of the second fact, at least,' Robert said, trying not to smile.

'Then perhaps you will stop trying to manage me,' Jack said, his voice gentle. 'Whatever happens to me is my choice, my fate alone. If you stop trying to take responsibility for it, we will both be better off.'

'You make that sound simpler than it is,' Robert replied, thinking of the morning he'd had.

'It will be easier, now that you have a wife,' Jack assured him. 'And soon you will have a family, as well.'

'What?'

His brother gave him a knowing smile. 'Lucy and I have not yet been blessed. But the gossip about the ballroom last night said that I should not be too secure in my inheritance, since you might have a son in a few months.'

'Then the gossip was mistaken,' he said. 'It was likely my mother-in-law who spread the rumours. And she is…premature in her hopes for us.' It was a far more charitable way to describe her than totally wrong.

'Hmmm,' Jack replied, obviously surprised with the dark look that Robert was giving him at what should have been good news.

'Too bad. But there is all the time in the world for that, isn't there?'

'Not for Beth, there wasn't,' Robert snapped.

'Next time, it will be different,' Jack assured him, with a confidence that showed how little he understood.

'I hope so.' It would be different, but only if he kept it from happening at all.

'And now, you should be going home,' his brother reminded him. 'We are all fine here and you have a wife who is probably waiting for that news. Tell her the ball was a great success, to keep her shoes on her feet and the windows closed against stray birds.'

'I will relay the message,' Robert said. Then he stood and walked towards the door.

Chapter Twenty-Two

Emma had slept barely at all that night for worrying about both her husband and the Major and Lucy. The servants had returned with the wagon after several hours and assured her that no one had been seriously hurt in the accident. It certainly was not the dire disaster that Robert had feared when he left.

But if that was true, why had he not returned home? When he had left the bedroom, it had been clear that he was about to have another spell. He had been in no condition to travel anywhere, much less ride off to rescue someone else. Suppose something had happened to him on the road that the servants were not aware of?

She was near to sending a party of footmen to search for him when she heard him coming in the front door of the manor. As she reached the head of the stairs, she saw him offer his greatcoat to the butler and walk down the hall to his study without bothering to look in her direction.

She hurried down the stairs and ran after him, following him into the room and closing the door behind them. 'Where have you been?'

He turned to her, and she saw lines of fatigue etched deep on his face. 'I did not think I needed your approval to visit with my brother.'

'Of course not,' she said, coming towards him. His shoulders slumped in exhaustion and she suspected he had had an attack at some point during the night, but she doubted he would want to discuss it. 'Was Jack all right? The servants said the accident was not severe.'

'He was well,' Robert said, 'As was his wife. Everything was fine.' But strangely, he did not seem happy with the fact.

'Then you admit that there was no reason to be as worried as you were when you left the house yesterday,' she prompted.

'My brother said much the same thing.' He sounded almost puzzled by the fact.

'You take too much upon yourself,' she said, linking her arm in his. 'I understand the need to assure yourself of Jack's safety. But you must trust that some things will work out for the best, if you just leave them alone,' she said.

'Perhaps,' he allowed.

'Then you admit that having a ball did not cause the accident?' she said.

'I am still not sure we should have done it,' he said.

'I am sorry,' she whispered. Some naive part of her was waiting for the old assurance that she had nothing to be sorry for, but it did not come. Apparently, the confidence of the previous evening had disappeared and they were slipping backwards into doubt and superstition. 'Perhaps it did not end as we wished it to. But yesterday, you said that the gathering itself was a success.'

'I thought so at the time,' he said. 'But apparently, your mother, who you allow to interfere in every element of our lives, was telling all and sundry at the ball last night that you are increasing. I had to correct my brother on the subject, but God only knows what the rest of the guests must believe.'

Everyone knew. Everyone but her husband, who still believed that they would be child-less, willing to ignore the evidence, simply because he wanted it to be so.

Now he had noted her silence. 'There is no truth in it, is there?'

He was waiting for her denial. When it did not come, he turned to her and laid his hand gently on her stomach. 'You are with child?' The exhaustion in his face changed to shock.

'There was always a risk that it would hap-pen,' she said. 'When we do the things we have been doing, it is not quite inevitable, but it is close to that.'

'But I have been so careful,' he said, shak-ing his head in confusion.

'Not the first time,' she reminded him. 'And do not lay this on the bad luck of the Gas-coynes.'

It was clear by the look on his face that it was exactly what he'd been thinking.

'Do not dare call the birth of our first child

a curse,' she said, almost shaking with anger. 'It is a blessing.'

'You know why I am upset,' he said, his voice taking on the cold rational tone he used to quell opposition.

'Because you think it means I will die?' She laughed. 'It is surprising that you care. I am sure your life would be much easier without me here to push you into doing things that you regret.'

'But that does not mean that I want you to die,' he responded, horrified.

'Then I won't,' she replied. 'There is no reason to believe I will, other than some names written in a book.'

'You are speaking of generations of my family history,' he snapped.

'History is in the past,' she reminded him. 'The future is what we make for ourselves. And I tell you, with my health and stamina, there is no reason I should not survive this, along with the child.'

'You have been sick already,' he countered, probably remembering how she had been after dancing that day in the ballroom.

'Those symptoms have already subsided,'

she said. 'They happen early in the process and that time has passed for me.'

'It has been that long,' he said, amazed. 'Then there is nothing to be done but to try to keep you safe for the duration of the pregnancy.'

She smiled, relieved that they were coming to an understanding.

'You must leave immediately,' he concluded, pacing the room as he made his plans.

'You are sending me away?' she said, shocked.

'It is not safe for you to be at Gascoyne Manor,' he replied, as if this made any sense at all. 'Or perhaps it is not safe for you to be near me.' His breathing was quickening as he spoke, becoming shallow and uneven.

'You are speaking of your foolish curse again,' she said, shaking her head.

'A foolish belief that has held true for five generations of wives,' he said.

'All the more reason that we will have no trouble. No one's bad luck holds indefinitely,' she said. 'And even you admitted that things have been going well for you since our marriage.'

'Until today,' he replied. 'Our happiness was too good to last for long. Today signals a turn back to the way things have always been for me. And I will not let my bad luck endanger you.'

'Then we will survive it together,' she said, trying another tack. 'If your luck truly is bad, surely it will be better if I am here to console you.'

'It is no consolation at all if I have you and happiness for a few months, only to lose you,' he said. 'I ignored my grandfather when he warned me what would happen to Elizabeth. But when she was in labour and most needed me to be strong for her, I had an attack and was a distraction instead of a help. Perhaps, if I had listened to him and sent her away, she would be alive today. I will not make that mistake again.'

'Your grandfather,' she said, scoffing. 'You have told me that you did not live with the man as you grew up.'

'I was not the one he kept,' Robert said, as if it still bothered him.

'Then you do not really know the man, do you?' she reminded him.

'And you did not meet him at all,' Robert reminded her.

'But I read his journals,' she said. 'And you have not.'

'I saw no need,' he said flatly.

'Then you do not really know who the man was that taught you to believe in a curse,' she said softly. 'Read them. You will understand that you have nothing to fear.'

'Nothing to fear?' He laughed bitterly. 'I have already seen what awaits me. Two graves and an empty place in both hearth and heart. I cannot… I will not go through that again.'

She went to him, then, reaching out a hand to comfort him.

But instead of accepting it, he shrugged it off and turned from her, refusing to meet her gaze. 'Perhaps you are right and all will be well with the birth. But you do not need me to help you through it. Since your mother always has a plan for you, let her figure this out. Pack your things and go back to her.'

'I cannot,' she said, feeling her new life collapsing around her. 'No matter what happens, I belong here with you.'

'You should have thought of that before you hid this child from me,' he said. 'I told you before the wedding that there would be no intimacy between us.'

'Do not blame me for a lie you told yourself,' she said, feeling her throat tighten with unshed tears.

'I agreed to marry you. I did not agree to anything else. That includes keeping you under my roof when it is clear that I cannot trust you to tell me the truth. Nor can I guarantee your safety, if you remain here. It is for the best if you go back to your parents' house for the duration of the pregnancy.'

'But I love you.' There. The words were out though she felt no better for having said them. And here was the moment where he could, at least, sweeten the pain of what was happening with a response of his own.

'I wish you did not,' he said, shaking his head. 'It only makes things more difficult.'

What had she expected, really? That a man who was so afraid of loss would give his heart again after losing it when his first wife had died.

'Very well,' she said. 'If you no longer want me, I will leave you.'

At this, his mouth opened, as if ready to argue. Then he closed it again.

'But I am not doing it to humour your foolishness. Nothing bad will happen to me, here or there. I can produce a family bible of my own, you see. It has both births and deaths in it, but there is nothing magical about the recording of facts. And there is no reason to believe that anything bad will happen to me. As my mother never fails to remind me, I am robust.' And God knew what she would say if Emma returned home to her with her marriage in shambles. After finally beginning to free herself from her mother's control, the thought of returning home as a failure was unbearable. She would have to find another place to stay.

She took a breath and continued. 'If you let me go now, do not think I will come back to you when the baby is born.'

'Why would you not?' he said and seemed honestly surprised that he could not dictate her comings and goings as if she was one of the servants.

She let out a moan of frustration. 'Because I no longer want to stay with a man who is incapable of love.'

'We have discussed this before,' he said.

'You have pontificated on your lack of belief in that emotion,' she said. 'But I would hardly call what we're having a discussion.'

'That is unfair,' he said.

'What is unfair is your pretending that you do not care about people when you obviously do. You love your brother and your fears for him caused an estrangement that lasted years. You loved your first wife and your baby. That is why you blame yourself for their deaths. And you are willing to believe in this elaborate charade of a curse, rather than admit that you work yourself into spells of panic when you cannot avoid the pain of loss that we all must sometimes experience.'

'Think what you like,' he said, obviously shaken by her assessment. 'But I do not want you here if there is any chance that it might end badly. When you have survived the birth you can return here and we will go back to the way we were.'

'But that is it,' she snapped. 'I do not want

things to be the way they were. I want more than that. I want a husband who loves me enough to face the bad with the good.'

'And I cannot give that to you,' he said, with a sigh. For a moment, he looked as though he might actually regret that he was not enough for her.

'Then we are in agreement,' she said, just as unhappy. 'I will leave. You will have your loneliness back and with it your peace of mind. I hope it gives you more joy than I could have.'

Chapter Twenty-Three

The house was empty again, just as it had been in the two years after Beth had died.

Then he had met Emma. It was amazing how quickly it had become full of joy and laughter, and her. Perhaps she was right that he had loved Beth, for he'd never really forgotten her. But the four months Emma had lived with him had flown past in a whirlwind of activity and he had forgotten there was another way to live.

The first evening without her was interminable and the next one even longer. It almost made him relent and beg her to come back. But then he remembered that her life and the life of a child were at stake. Just the thought of what might happen made his heart race until it felt as though it might explode.

He was able to calm himself by remembering that she'd told him she would not be returning, no matter what he did. To get her to even consider it would require more than he was capable of giving her. But with that calm had come a lingering sadness deeper than any he had felt before.

It was both good and bad to know that she was safe. He regretted that he had sent her back to a home which had crushed her spirit and her soul during the time she'd lived in it. Was she even now returning to the hesitant girl that had walked down the aisle with him? Or could she manage to keep the confidence that had grown in her while they had been together?

It was better that he did not know, for if he did not like the truth, he might be tempted to drag her back, no matter the consequences for either of them. So he did nothing.

But some things were easier because of it. He was no longer happy, but neither did he have paralysing spells of doubt. His heartbeat was steady, unmoved by fear or passion. His hands were warm and steady, but no one held them as he drifted off to sleep. He did not feel love, but neither did he feel pain.

* * *

The months passed in peace. He caught up on his reading. He rode less and slept more. He stopped dressing for dinner, since there was no one there to see him. And when he played tennis, which was seldom, he did it in the tennis court, unable to bring himself to enter the ballroom, even if it was not being used for its intended purpose.

He avoided the neighbours, just as he used to. In return, no one visited him. It was unexpected when the butler announced that Major Gascoyne had come, but Robert hardly had the energy to be surprised by it. 'Show him in.'

His brother entered, staring at him critically, noting his untrimmed hair and stubble with a sigh. 'Hello, Robert.'

'Hello, Jack,' he replied. 'Come to borrow money?'

His brother laughed. 'Do not think you can bait me into one of our old arguments that easily. Even though your wife is gone, I would hope that some of her influence on your manners will remain.'

'What makes you think my wife is gone?'

Robert asked, rubbing his unshaven cheek and wondering if it was possible to keep a secret in this community or if Emma had announced his betrayal to the world.

'Because she has been living in my house for weeks.' Jack shook his head. 'Did you honestly try to send her home? Surely you must have realised that she would not go there, of all places.'

'I did not think she would go to you,' he said, surprised.

'We are the only other family she has,' Jack replied. 'And she and Lucy have grown quite close now that they are both increasing.'

'I am sorry to impose my problems on you,' Robert said.

'And congratulations to you, as well,' Jack said, as if to remind him what the correct response to such news should be.

'I will accept your congratulations after the child and the mother is safe,' he replied.

'Because, apparently, you believe she is unsafe in her own home,' Jack said, shaking his head. 'And all because of something our mad grandfather told you.'

Mad? Was Jack serious or exaggerating?

And what was it that Emma had said about not really knowing the man until he had read the journals? Perhaps insanity ran in their family.

Robert nodded. Then it was no surprise that he was mad as well. 'I know the idea is ludicrous. But I also remember what happened to Elizabeth. I am willing to sacrifice anything to prevent even the smallest chance that it will happen again.'

'If it happens, then it will be in my house and you will not have to see it,' Jack said. 'That is not a matter of keeping her safe, that is an act of cowardice on your part.'

'Perhaps it is,' Robert agreed. 'But not all of us are as brave as you, little brother.'

At this, Jack gave a short, bitter laugh. 'Bravery is a relative thing. In your case, I suspect you would rather face an army single-handed than see your wife hurt. And she, in turn, will not come home until you have the nerve to keep her.'

'Then I will have to learn to live without her, just as she is learning to do without me,' he said. And it must have been the right decision, for just the thought of what might be coming made his head swim and his hands grow cold.

'I will inform you when the child is born,' Jack said, disgusted, rising to go. 'Then, we will see if either of you has come to your senses. For now, I will leave you on your own, just as you wish to be.'

Once he was gone, Robert was left to his thoughts, which were more confused than ever. It was some comfort to know that Emma was safe and happy in Jack's home and that all was going well so far. But it was clear that Jack did not take the family curse any more seriously than his wife did.

Which raised the question of why Robert believed something that his brother knew nothing of. On the rare times he'd bothered to talk to him, his grandfather had been adamant that the family was doomed. Perhaps it was some secret that was only shared with the heir, though the old man had left no instructions as to secrecy when he had died.

Or, perhaps it was a story to frighten children into obedience and it had simply got out of hand. But that could not be right, for there had been no promise that good behaviour would mitigate the effects of the tragedy Grandfather had promised him. It had certainly done him no good, for his disabling spells had grown worse after each of his grandfather's warnings, as if to prove the curse's existence.

Perhaps it was time to heed Emma's final warning to him and read what she had found in his grandfather's writings. He went to the study, where the journals and diaries of the previous masters of the house were kept. If there was a curse, as his grandfather had said, surely there must be some point, in the past, where it had started. He could not find a way to end it if he did not know how it began.

His grandfather had spoken as if it were always there, immutable for generations. How far back must he look? Fifty years? A hundred? At last he decided to start one generation back, with his great-grandfather, and work slowly back from there.

But after an evening's skimming of ten years of stewardship of the property, he could find no mention at all of a problem. Things happened, both good and bad, and they were recorded in the same, even hand as if the writer was untouched by the event to any great degree. And through it all, there was no mention of any kind of supernatural influence on events.

Then he turned to his grandfather's journals. They, too, started out in the same even tone as his predecessor. But after the death of his second wife, the narrative began to unravel. His grandfather had begun to look back through the journals of his ancestors, just as Robert was doing. But his read on them was quite different. He focused on the negative to the exclusion of all else. And as he did so, he searched for a pattern to justify them.

Slowly, month by month, his grandfather's writing lost any sense of perspective. He wrote only of the disasters that befell him and his family. There was not a trace of light left in the narrative, even at times that Robert knew had been successful and prosperous for the family.

And this was the man he had listened to, in the formative years of his life. He had ignored the man for as long as he could. But after Beth's death, every conversation had come back to him and the family curse had become as real to him as the walls and floor of the house.

But apparently, the whole thing had come from the tortured mind of a grieving man. It had made him wallow in his own grief and turn from possibilities that might have succeeded, out of fear of inevitable failure.

Worse yet, he had turned from the one woman who had offered to change his life, sending her away. He could call her back and make it right. He should go to her right now and tell her that he had been wrong. But as he walked towards the door, his knees went weak and his blood turned to ice. Before he had been able to summon a servant to get his horse, he had gone back to his study, poured a brandy and taken a chair.

Suppose he was wrong? In this, of all things, would it be harmful to wait just a few months to be sure that she and the baby would be safe? And what if they were not safe, even at his brother's house? What if there was no curse, but she died anyway?

It was then that his heart began to pound in earnest. He gripped the edge of the desk with his fingertips, holding so tight that he was sure he must be leaving dents in the wood. The only good thing about the departure of Emma was that he had been largely free of these spells, confident that he was doing what was best for her, trying to keep her safe.

But if there was no curse, then there was nothing he could do, one way or the other, to influence the future. He had no way to control what was happening around him. And with that, the terror hit him, washing over him in a wave.

When it had passed, he sat weak and drained. Even if he wanted to, he could not go to her like this. Until he found a way to master his spirit, he was no good for her, now or in the future.

Chapter Twenty-Four

Her time was coming soon. Emma could still not believe that the months had passed so quickly, especially since she had been doing nothing more than reading novels and waiting for a visitor that would not come.

The Major had been to visit his brother and had little to say on his return, other than that the man was a stubborn fool. It annoyed Emma that the truce between the two of them had evaporated along with her marriage. It was even worse that, by coming here, she felt she had taken the wrong side in an argument she wanted no part of.

But what else was she to do? She was not welcome to go home to her husband, even if she had wanted to. And it was clear, after Jack's visit, that Robert would not come to get her.

Now, Lucy appeared in the doorway of her room and offered her a letter. 'It is from your husband,' she said.

'Really,' she said and took it, unsure of what her reaction ought to be after four months of silence. She slit the seal and unfolded it to read.

Dear Emma,

Much has happened since you've been away that might be of interest to you.

I have had more news from Cornwall on the mine I invested in. Though it was a failure before we married, since then it has been producing at an astounding rate. The profits have been far more than I hoped for when I invested.

In addition, it seems that our mutual friend, Hercules the bull, managed to find a weak spot in the fence and spent the day rampaging over the countryside. No one was hurt during the escape, but a herd of neighbouring cows will likely be doubled come spring. The farmer is as yet unsure whether to complain or to pay me a stud fee.

The servants are rebuilding the bull en-closure as we speak, to be sure that any further trips off the property will not be impromptu.

I must apologise for my complaints of cursed luck on the day you left me. It was an overreaction on my part, as was any blame you might think I have placed on you.

'What does he say?' Lucy asked, leaning forward.

'Apparently, he wishes to tell me how well he is doing without me,' Emma said with a disappointed sniff, and continued reading.

As you suggested, I read my grandfa-ther's journals and understand what you were trying to tell me about the state of his mind. It was clear that the curse was an invention of his own tortured brain. But, although I am attempting to, it has been difficult for me to release what I be-lieved for so many years.

Though I blamed the curse for the spells that sometimes affect me, it is clear that they are a part of me and not something that is likely to end by dint of effort or a change in luck. And unfortunately I am still overcome at the thought of your impending delivery.

Though I endeavour to be better, I fear I am still not the man you deserve. I think of you always and miss you each day and each night. But I do not want to call you back to me, where you belong, only to fail you when you need me most.
Sincerely,
Robert

Emma shook the paper, as if it were possible to change the words on it by force. 'It is both better and worse than I hoped. He finally admits that his curse is nonsense, but still does not feel that he is worthy of me.' She stared back at Lucy. 'And he signs with sincerity and not with love. What am I to do with a man like that?'

Lucy could offer nothing more than a shrug and a shake of her head.

When the first pain came, two weeks later, it was hardly a pain at all. Emma was sitting in Major Gascoyne's garden working listlessly at a watercolour of a flower, when her body rebelled. Suddenly, the muscles of her stomach became hard as stone. Everything seemed to freeze inside her, as if time itself had stopped. And then, as quickly as it had come, the pain disappeared.

She was going to have a baby. She had known that fact for months, yet, it had not become true to her until this moment. Had she thought that the process would somehow resolve itself without this most difficult of acts?

Now that the time was here, it was all wrong. No matter that she had been here almost as long as she had been with Robert, this was not her home. She could not have a baby in a stranger's house. Lucy, great friend that she had been, knew nothing about pregnancy or birth. Despite the house being full of people, she could not think of a single one that could help her at this moment.

But what did that leave her? She could not imagine going back to her parents' home at this time, only to be guided through the duration of the long hours by her mother. It was very likely that she would be given a litany of her faults, while trying to do what any woman was designed by God to be capable of.

But she could not go home. The man she loved had turned her away and did not think he had the courage to face this moment. He said he had done it for her own good, but he had abandoned her. It was the sort of thing that happened to fallen women, not to wives. They were not supposed to be homeless and unloved when about to deliver a possible heir. He claimed to have her welfare at heart, but was it not just as likely that she would die in the care of strangers and not in her own bed?

She did not want that. In the short time she had been there, Gascoyne Manor had been all that she had wanted. A place where she had been free and safe from criticism. For the first time in her life, she had felt normal. She had not had to change herself to fit the world. The world had been subtly adjusted to suit her. And it was all because of the man she loved, whose baby she was about to have.

Perhaps he was convinced that he would be of no use to her, but right now she did not need her mother or her sister-in-law. She needed her husband.

She set her paints aside and took a deep breath, waiting to see if it was followed by another pain. When none came, she stood up and set out for home.

Chapter Twenty-Five

Robert was in his study when the knock on the front door came.

Such things were obvious in the house, which had grown quiet as a tomb, just as it used to be before Emma had come into his life. Then he had not noticed how depressing the silence was. It had not bothered him as it did now. But the single sound of a knock could bring him starting out of his chair and out into the hall to find the reason for the disturbance.

He could hear the commotion in the hall before he arrived. The servants were in an uproar and the butler was calling for footmen to calm themselves and find the master.

'Here,' he said, as the knot of people parted to reveal his wife, sagging in the arms of his housekeeper.

He pushed the older woman out of the way and wrapped his arms around his wife, feeling her body go rigid in his arms as a pain took her. 'Emma,' he said, confused.

'I came home,' she said, weaving on her feet as if she did not quite know where she was.

'But how?'

'I walked,' she said, grimacing. 'It is not far. You would have discovered it yourself if you had bothered to visit me in all this time.' Then she slipped away from him and doubled over, her hands over her bulging abdomen.

'I wanted you to be safe,' he said. It was an inadequate excuse and a part of him no longer believed it. He had not gone to her because she made him feel too much. And when those feelings went wrong, it hurt too much to bear.

'Well, I am here now,' she said. 'Where I belong.'

He felt the first, traitorous palpitations of his heart. 'You belong far away from here until after the baby is gone,' he said. 'I will call for the carriage.'

At this, the housekeeper gave a huff of disapproval. 'She is in no condition to go anywhere but her room, Sir Robert.'

She could not stay here. Just the sight of her bulging belly brought back memories that he had spent years trying to bury. He could hear Beth's screams echoing in his head as his heart began to race.

When he did not respond, the housekeeper added, 'It is her time', with a significance that could not be ignored.

'No,' he said, as if his wishes could make any difference to the outcome. 'She walked here from my brother's home. Surely, if she were in labour...'

Now, the housekeeper looked at him with exasperation, clearly tired of all men and him in particular. 'Women in the throes of childbirth can be irrational. She wanted to be here, so she came.'

This was the worst place for her. It had been the wrong place for her when she had fallen in that ditch, but on that day, he had brought her here without thinking twice. Why had he not been smarter from the first? But that was long ago and now it was too late to send her away.

'We will make her comfortable in her room,' the housekeeper said, holding out her arms to take his wife.

'If anyone is to do that, it will be me,' he said, reaching for her as she doubled over again. He braced her body against his and put his hands on her shoulders, rubbing slowly until he felt the muscles begin to relax. And as her breathing returned to normal, so did his.

She looked up at him in amazed relief. 'Thank you.'

'It will not help for long, I fear,' he said. Then, he scooped an arm beneath her knees and lifted her into his arms.

'I can walk,' she murmured, though she barely struggled in his arms.

'I want to carry you,' he replied, surprised to find it true. Now, of all times, he needed to touch her, to feel that she was real. The weight of her in his arms was calming and he felt his strength begin to return. Then he carried her up the stairs and down the hall, laying her on her own bed just as another pain struck her and curled her long frame into a ball.

He felt the gentle touch of the housekeeper on his sleeve, trying to pull him away. 'A lunch will be laid for you in the study.'

Why was she trying to calm him with food? He could not possibly think to eat at a time like this. 'That will not be necessary,' he said, reaching to take Emma's hand and feeling her grip tighten on his fingers until he thought she would break them.

'The doctor has been summoned,' the housekeeper replied, trying to tug him away. 'There is nothing more for you to do except wait.'

'Wait,' he said numbly. 'For how long?'

'For as long as it takes,' she explained, her mouth quirking in the barest of smiles. 'But I would expect that, for a first child, it will be the better part of a full day.'

'A day,' he repeated, for suddenly he could not manage anything other than to parrot the words spoken to him.

'We will come for you when the baby is born,' she promised him.

'I don't want to leave you,' he said, looking into the frightened eyes of his wife and raising her hand to his lips so he could kiss the knuckles.

'It will be all right,' she said in a surprisingly firm tone. 'Everything will be fine, just as I promised. They will come for you when it is over.'

Since he was not wanted in the birthing room, he walked to his study, numb with the weight of her words. He did not want it to be over. The time he had spent with Emma had been the most delightful months of his life. And now it might end in disaster.

Or it might not, he reminded himself. She had never believed in the curse, the last dregs of which still clouded his common sense. Perhaps, since it was never real to her, it could not hurt her. Or perhaps his belief in disaster was strong enough for both of them. Perhaps he could bring disaster down upon them, just with his doubt.

The thought was like a canker in his heart, lodged and growing there. He must pluck it out. Just as it was not sensible to believe in Grandfather's curse, it was not logical that he could create the disaster he most feared, just by thinking of it.

He must change the way he was used to seeing the world and he must do so quickly, for Emma's sake and his own. He sat down at his desk and emptied his head of disastrous imaginings, telling himself firmly that there would be nothing unusual about this birth.

But that was easier to do, before the screaming started. He could hear Emma crying out above, the screams of pain echoing through the house. Each one was like a knife in his heart, as he compared them to those of a different woman, praying for some sign that things were going better.

He had done this to them both with his careless willingness to succumb to carnal desire. It was too late for Beth, but Emma might survive. Yet he had already failed her. He had been willing to let her suffer alone at his brother's home because he was too weak to go to her.

For the first time in his life, he prayed and not in the casual way one did during the dreary Sunday sermons of the vicar. He spoke to God directly, willing to beg, willing to barter. He made so many promises that he could not remember what they were, but he would keep them all if the day ended without tragedy.

Lunch turned to dinner and the cries did not end. They intensified. He sent for the housekeeper, demanding news, but she had none to offer other than that things were going as well as could be expected. But what did that mean? And was it his imagination, or was there a trace of doubt on her face as she said it?

'I want to see her,' he announced.

'I do not think that is wise,' she said, shaking her head.

'When you are master of this house, you can make the decisions,' he said, forcing his fear back down into his belly. 'There is something I must say to her.'

'Very well,' she said. 'But I cannot promise the response you will get.'

It might not matter, since he could not guarantee that he had the strength to make it up the stairs to her. But the effort had to be made.

He made it as far as the study door before his heart began to pound. He paused, clutching the door frame. It was bad enough to be a homebound prisoner of his own moods. He would not allow them to limit him to a single room. He closed his eyes for a moment and forced his breathing to slow, counting between inhales and exhales, until he felt less lightheaded. Then he continued down the hall to the foot of the stairs.

Emma's cries were louder there and, for a moment, he lost heart again, grabbing the banister and fighting down another wave of irrational panic. Then he locked his gaze on the head of the stairs and focused his mind on the happy times they'd had since he had found her.

Tennis. Dancing. Galloping together. Making love. So many joyful times. He found a different memory for each step, until he had reached the top. Now he was in the upper hallway which seemed incredibly long. Each step was a struggle, growing even harder as he neared the woman crying out in pain. He kept going, conquering his fear until his cold hand was on the door handle of her room.

When he opened the door his beautiful wife's face was contorted with pain and dripping sweat. 'What do you want?' she snarled in a voice he had never heard before.

For a moment, he was taken aback. He had struggled and won for a woman who clearly did not want him anywhere near. But then he remembered the illogical walk she had made and the housekeeper's explanation for it.

'Sir Robert, you should not be here.' The same doctor who attended his first wife's unfortunate labour was here to help Emma. And it alarmed him to notice that, just as Harris had said when they first met, the man was clearly in his cups, smelling of gin and in no condition to help a woman in need.

'I will be the judge of where I should and should not be,' he said, staring the man down until he had backed away from the door and allowed Robert into the room.

Then he looked to the woman in the bed and focused on her strength and courage, took a deep breath and announced, 'I needed to tell you that I love you.'

'What?' she roared.

'I love you,' he repeated, enjoying the sound of the words.

'And you decide to tell me that now,' she snapped. Then she was taken by another pain, and the last word dragged into a long, high-pitched *ow*...

'I thought...'

'You thought to tell me, before I died?' This was followed by a mad laugh.

'No,' he insisted. 'I should not have waited so long to say it. I should have told you before you left me. I loved you then and I love you now.'

'Then tell me again, after I have your child,' she shouted. 'I am going to have this baby and we will both be fine,' she added, though it ended in another wail of pain. 'Now, get out! And take that drunken quack with you.' Then his mild-mannered wife grabbed the water carafe from the table at bedside and pitched it at the doctor's head.

'My lady, I must insist,' the surgeon said in a weak voice.

Robert looked to the housekeeper for confirmation, and she whispered that the doctor was not technically needed.

He smiled and nodded. This, at least, was something he could do to help. He looked back to his wife and assured her, 'I will take care of it.' He grabbed the other man's arm and retreated to the hall. Then he paid the fellow and sent him on his way.

When he came back, he did not bother returning to the study, for he could no longer bear waiting for word to reach him on the ground floor. Instead, he climbed the stairs again and paced the upper hall, stopping each time he passed it to lay his hand on the wood of her bedroom door, willing his strength into her.

Gradually, the screams turned to groans. As he reached the end of the hall for what seemed like the thousandth time, all sound stopped from the room. As he rushed back to the door, the ominous silence was split by the squall of an infant.

Now his heart was beating hard again, but as if it could not contain the joy inside it. It made him wonder why he had wasted years avoiding a thing which gave him such pleasure.

The door opened and the housekeeper

stepped in front of him as he tried to rush into the room, pressing a hand firmly to the centre of his chest as he tried to enter. 'Mother and baby are fine. A few minutes more, and you may see them,' she said.

'Let him come,' a voice called from the bedroom. Emma sounded strong and triumphant. And when he went to her, though she was obviously exhausted her eyes were clear and her smile the same as ever.

And there, on the bed beside her, was a small pink miracle wrapped in flannel. 'May I introduce you to your daughter, Sir Robert,' his wife said with a smile.

He stared down at the baby, all pink squirming flesh and bright eyes, and still could not imagine that it had come and that he'd had any part in the making of something—no, *someone* so wonderful. He held out a tentative finger, nudging the hand that was tangled in the blanket, and felt the fingers close on his in a tiny fist.

'Her name is Rosamunde,' Emma said.

He felt his heart give another, strong answering thump to the sound of his wife's voice, which was, if possible, even more commanding than when she had shouted at him. 'Since you were so convinced that she would not live and could not seem to be bothered, I took the liberty of choosing names while I was at the Major's house.' The words gentled somewhat at the end of the sentence, but only a little.

'You took a great risk in coming here,' he said hoarsely. 'Suppose you had been hurt on the way?'

'Because I am the sort of clumsy girl that falls into ditches because she does not watch where she is going? Or was that because of the curse?' she pressed, giving him no quarter at all in what now felt like foolishness.

'You are not clumsy,' he said. 'In fact, you are quite graceful when you put your mind to being so. And as for the curse? I admit to being…overly cautious,' he said. 'But you cannot blame me at being terrified by the possibility of losing you.' He shook free of his daughter's grip and sat down on the edge of the bed, taking his wife's hand. 'What would I have done without you?'

'I suspect you would have found something,' she said, her voice gruff. 'You still might, you know.'

'Do not say that you mean to leave, now that you have come back to me,' he said.

'I will stay,' she assured him. 'But I cannot swear to you that I will outlive you.'

'Do not speak of such a thing,' he said, gathering up her hands and burying his face in them, kissing the palms. 'We will both die together, many years from now, at a very old age.'

'You know that, do you?' she replied, her smile turning saucy.

'I cannot imagine it any other way,' he replied. 'If I were to lose you now, I think I should run mad. And as you must have noticed by now, I am not far from madness already.'

'As always, you are far too dramatic,' she said with a kind smile. 'It is because you care deeply about the people around you that you are sometimes overcome with emotion. I can hardly fault you for loving me too much.'

'And since you said before that you wished to hear it again, I do love you and missed you terribly while you were gone.'

'Please, tell me about it,' she said, sagging back in the bed pillows, exhausted. 'I have had a long day and am in the mood to be flattered by you,' she commanded him with a confidence that she had not had when he married her, and that made him love her all the more.

'I missed your beauty.' He kissed her hands again. 'Your wit. Your ceaseless optimism.' He leaned closer and whispered in her ear, 'And taking you against that tree. I most assuredly want to do that again.'

She laughed and it was strong and healthy, and he felt the last of his fear slipping away. 'I was the luckiest man in the world when I found you,' he said.

'It's about time you realised that,' she said, pulling him close for a kiss.

* * * * *